LOVE LETTERS

Shireen and Michael would love to spend the whole summer together. But Michael has to go on an exchange trip — to Madrid. As the weeks zoom by and he finally leaves, Shireen only has his letters to look forward to . . . But taking Michael's place at home is irresistible Pedro, the Spanish exchange student. Shireen really loves Michael, but he's so far away and Pedro is right there . . . Lonely and confused, Shireen writes a letter to Spain . . . But is it what Michael wants to hear?

Point R♥mance

LOVE LETTERS

Denise Colby

Complete and Unabridged

spectrum
LARGE PRINT

First published in Great Britain in 1997 by
Scholastic Children's Books
London

First Large Print Edition
published 2000
by arrangement with
Scholastic Children's Books
London

British Library CIP Data

Colby, Denise
  Love letters.—Large print ed.—
  (Point romance)—Spectrum imprint
  1. Love stories
  2. Young adult fiction
  3. Large type books
  I. Title
  823.9′14 [J]

  ISBN 0–7089–9514–4

Published by
F. A. Thorpe (Publishing)
Anstey, Leicestershire

Set by Words & Graphics Ltd.
Anstey, Leicestershire
Printed and bound in Great Britain by
T. J. International Ltd., Padstow, Cornwall

This book is printed on acid-free paper

To Denis Bond

1

Shireen gazed from the third-floor Art Room window and down towards the grass courts where the year-twelve boys were on the last round of their tennis tournament. Taking out a Kleenex from the pocket of her white blouse, she pushed back her blonde fringe and gently dabbed the sweat from her forehead. It was the hottest July she'd known; uncomfortably hot . . . and yet, when most of the pupils at Melthorn High were looking forward to the end of term and their trips to the coast and open-air pools, Shireen had no such longings.

Her place at college had been secured but, unable to find a temporary job, she'd decided to remain at school, helping Alison to design the set for next term's pantomime.

Alison approached and stood beside her, smiling knowingly. 'I bet I know who you're watching,' she said. 'That's the *real* reason you stayed on at school.'

Shireen smiled too, her eyes never

leaving the handsome figure leaping around the tennis court, his blond hair flapping across his stunningly bright blue eyes. She sighed. 'Yes. Pity he doesn't know I exist,' she replied.

Alison placed an arm around her best friend's shoulder. 'Of course he does, Shireen,' she said, softly. 'Michael's just shy, that's all. I mean, have you ever seen him talking to *any* of the girls?'

This was precisely why Shireen had taken a shine to the handsome, sporty lad. He wasn't pushy, like so many of the other boys in year twelve. Throughout the year, many of them had approached both her and Alison to ask them out. But then that seemed to be almost customary at Melthorn High. The year-twelve boys would date the year-eleven girls. And even though these boys were only one year older, they always appeared to be so confident.

'Why don't *you* ask *him* for a date?' suggested Alison, with a broad grin. 'After all, you haven't got long. Three weeks. Then you may never see him again.'

'I know. I know,' sighed Shireen, fearfully. 'Don't remind me.'

Miss Butler, the art teacher, entered the

class and saw the two girls staring through the window. She crossed to them and followed their gaze across the tennis court. All three watched as the stocky, blond lad, dressed in white shorts and T-shirt, thundered across the court and whacked the ball straight into the net.

'There's a lot to do, girls,' Miss Butler said softly. 'Time to take your eyes off the boys, eh?'

In the distance, Michael turned and looked up at the sky, noting the clouds just beginning to eclipse the sun. Shireen and Alison leapt back from the window with a squeal. They wondered if they'd been seen, staring down at him. They followed the squeal with a burst of giggles.

Miss Butler gave them a mock scowl. 'Come on, girls,' she said. 'Let's get on with these designs. You can continue boy-watching at lunchtime.'

★ ★ ★

Gavin held back his head and opened his mouth, filling it with the warm water running from the communal shower until his cheeks swelled to bursting. Michael glanced sideways at his best friend who was, as usual, acting the fool.

'Aren't you ever going to grow up, Gavin?' grinned Michael as he ran the soap over his tanned chest.

Gavin squirted the water into the air and laughed as it sprayed over the shower ceiling and down on to his head. 'I'll grow up when I leave here,' he said. 'When I have to get up at six in the morning and go off to work.'

Michael turned to face the tall, slim boy, handing him the bar of soap. 'I thought you were going off to university?' he said. 'So, what's changed?'

Gavin took the soap and rubbed it with gusto into his spiky red hair. 'Well, it depends, doesn't it? If I don't get the grades then I can't, can I? I'll have to work in my dad's garage instead.'

Michael grimaced at the thought. He hated anything to do with cars and he could never understand how Gavin could get so excited about fiddling with engines and getting covered with oil.

'I'm not Mr Brainbox, like you,' Gavin went on. 'I shall probably fail the lot.'

Michael turned off the shower and reached for his towel. 'Of course you won't. I bet you end up with better grades than me.' He began to roughly dry his blond hair. 'Then you'll be off to university . . . and still be acting like a ten-year-old.'

Gavin also grabbed for a towel and began drying himself. 'Still, one thing's for sure,' he said. 'I'm a better tennis player than you.'

Michael laughed loudly. 'Give over! I won the match.'

'Aah, but only because the sun was in my eyes,' Gavin grinned. 'It was glinting off the Art Room window.'

Michael playfully flicked him with his towel. 'Bad loser,' he said. He left the shower and crossed into the changing-room where his clothes hung on a peg.

Gavin followed him. 'I bet you didn't see *her*, either, did you?'

'Who?' asked Michael. He sat on the bench below his peg and began to dry his toes.

'Shireen.'

'Shireen?' Michael's heart began to race.

'She was watching me . . . thrashing *you* out on the court.'

'Give over.'

'Honest,' said Gavin. 'She was staring out of the Art Room window. Her and her friend. That Alison with the long black hair.'

'But who says she was watching *me*?' asked Michael.

Gavin shrugged and grinned. 'Yeah. Perhaps it's me she's after. Let's face it, I'm sure she'd prefer a tall lanky ginger-nut to someone like you.' For a few seconds his eyes saddened. He knew there was no way he could ever compete in the romance-stakes with someone as good-looking as Michael.

'I really like her, Gavin,' Michael said, seriously. 'I think she's beautiful.' He reached for his shirt and began to get dressed. 'I wish I could talk to her,' he added.

Gavin lectured his best friend: 'Be bold. Just go up to her and ask her out. You can take her to a movie . . . or McDonald's, or . . . well, *anywhere*. But if you don't ask her soon, then you've had it! She's leaving school in three weeks.'

The lunchtime pips sounded over the gym's speakers.

'Great,' said Gavin. 'I'm starving. Are you having a school lunch today?'

'Yes,' Michael replied softly. He wondered if Shireen would be in the dining-hall. And he wondered if he could summon up the courage to sit at her table.

⋆ ⋆ ⋆

'Don't look now!' Alison mumbled through a mouthful of pizza, as she peered through her black fringe. 'He's just come in with Gavin; that tall, ginger-haired boy.'

Shireen flicked a sideways glance across the dining-hall towards the main door and saw Michael heading for the serving-hatch.

'Perhaps he'll come and sit here,' added Alison. 'And then you've *got* to say something to him.'

Two year-nine boys approached and plonked down their trays on to the girls' table.

'We're saving those seats,' Alison said sharply. 'Hop it.'

One of the boys sneered. 'You can't save seats. It's not allowed.' He took his place opposite Shireen and began to fork up his dinner. Then he looked across and gave her a cheeky grin. 'Want one?' he asked, offering her a soggy chip, dangling from the end of his fork. 'I've put vinegar on it.'

Shireen giggled. 'No thanks,' she replied, kindly.

Alison stared at the boy who was about to offer *her* a chip. 'No!' she said aggressively before he had time to speak. 'Can't you go and sit with kids your own age?'

The boy placed the chip in his mouth and smirked at her.

'Too late,' sighed Gavin as he and Michael turned from the serving-hatch carrying their wooden trays. 'I thought that was our chance. We could've sat with them. Then you'd *have* to say something to her.'

Michael smiled, resignedly. 'Another day,' he said.

He and Gavin sat at an empty table on the other side of the dining-hall and began to eat.

'Give her a look,' said Gavin. 'She'll never know you're interested unless you make it obvious.'

Michael attempted a quick glance across the hall, but as he did so, Shireen reached out for the pepper-pot and missed his faltering advances.

Alison nearly choked on her pizza. 'He looked at you,' she said. 'He looked straight over here. He *does* know you exist. I *told* you.'

Urged on by Gavin, Michael looked across again, this time catching Shireen's eye.

Shireen returned the look with a coy smile . . . and Michael quickly looked away. The fork in his hand was trembling as he scooped up a small amount of coleslaw.

Gavin was amazed. 'You're shaking,' he gasped.

Michael felt very embarrassed. His face began to redden. 'My arm's just a bit shaky from holding the tennis racket,' he lied.

Gavin's eyes twinkled. 'You sure?' he said.

Michael rapidly began to down his food. 'Come on,' he said. 'Let's get some sun on our bodies. It's stupid sitting around in here.'

'Do you want me to go over and tell her?' asked Gavin.

'Tell her what?'

'That you fancy her and that you want to take her out.'

Michael was horrified. 'Give over!' he said. 'I hate all that 'my friend fancies you' stuff. It's humiliating.'

'Shall I go over and say something?' asked Alison.

'Like what?' asked Shireen.

'Like you think he's the most gorgeous bloke in the school.'

'You dare!' Shireen warned her. 'If I decide to chat him up, I'll do it without your help, thank you, Alison.'

The year-nine boy grinned at her through a mouthful of tomato-ketchup-soaked burger. 'You can chat *me* up if you like,' he said, sounding half-serious. Then he added, 'Go on. Have a chip.'

* * *

Michael took off his shirt and lay on his back. Most of the upper-school students who used these old amphitheatre steps beyond the tennis courts for sunbathing during the summer term, were silently reading.

'You should take yours off too, Gavin,' Michael said. 'Get some sun to that pale skin of yours.'

'I can't,' replied Gavin, irritably. 'You know I burn.' He enviously eyed Michael's golden chest and stomach. 'You don't realize how lucky you are,' he sighed. 'I wish I could tan like that. I just go all pink.'

'It's a good job you're not coming to Spain with me then, isn't it?' said Michael. 'I can't wait to get there.'

Gavin shrugged. 'I'd be better holidaying in Iceland,' he said. 'With a bag over my head.'

Michael laughed.

'You'll be all burnt up to a little cinder if you lie out like this in Spain,' Gavin warned him. 'It's dangerous, you know. People going on holiday abroad are always being warned.'

Michael turned on his side and leaned up on one elbow, facing Gavin. 'How many more times?' he said. 'I'm not going on holiday. I'm going to study. I won't even see a beach where I'm staying.'

'It's a pity she won't see you when you get back, looking like Adonis, isn't it?' smiled Gavin.

'Shireen?'

'Yes. She'll be doing some dead-end nine-to-five job somewhere, I expect,' he continued. 'She'll be earning a wage and going out with some guy she works with by then.' He laughed. 'Like a proper grown-up! Not like you and me . . . the eternal students of Melthorn High.'

'She might be going to college,' said Michael. He sat up. 'Are you absolutely sure she's not coming back to do her A-levels?'

'She's definitely leaving,' Gavin assured him. 'I've been asking around.'

Michael eyed him suspiciously. 'You sound as though you're pretty interested in her yourself.'

'I was asking for *you*,' Gavin grinned. 'I thought you'd want to know.' He stopped suddenly, tightly gripping Michael's arm. 'She's over by the tennis courts,' he said. 'She's coming this way.'

Michael immediately lay on his back again.

'What are you doing?' hissed Gavin.

'Playing cool,' Michael replied.

'Playing cool?' Gavin gasped in disbelief. 'Freezing her out, more like. Don't be stupid. You'll never get to talk to her at this rate.' He could see the pulse beating in Michael's bare chest. 'You're scared stiff!' he added.

Michael quickly sat up again. 'No, I'm not!' he said, defiantly.

To Gavin's surprise, he got to his feet

and, holding his rolled shirt in his hand, he began to head towards Shireen and Alison.

Alison croaked, 'He's walking towards us!'

Shireen turned and began to walk back towards the upper-school entrance.

Alison followed close on her heels. 'I don't believe you!' she snapped. 'He obviously wants to talk. Why are you running away?'

Shireen quickened her pace. 'I can't, Alison,' she said, looking back over her shoulder. 'I don't know what to say to him.'

Michael stopped in his tracks and stared after the two girls. He turned and dispiritedly strolled back to where Gavin sat, open-mouthed.

'What happened there?' asked Gavin.

Michael sat. 'I don't know. She saw me and just sped away.'

'Perhaps she's as nervous as you,' suggested Gavin.

'Give over,' replied Michael. 'It's obvious, Gavin. She just doesn't fancy me.'

He lay on his back, closed his eyes and felt the warm rays of the sun burning into his reddening cheeks.

★ ★ ★

Half-way through the afternoon, Gavin found Michael in the library, engrossed in a Spanish verb book. He sat beside him and whispered, so as not to disturb the other A-level students around them. 'I've got an idea.'

Michael closed his book. 'Tell me.'

'A letter,' said Gavin. 'You can write her a letter.'

Michael sighed. 'A love letter? Give over, Gavin.'

'What's wrong with that?' asked Gavin. 'You know how good you are at English. Write her a letter, asking her out . . . and we can leave it in her form-room desk.'

Michael shook his head, unsure. 'I don't know.'

'Go on,' Gavin urged him. 'Look, I'll help you to write it.' He began to sound excited. 'We can keep it simple. You haven't got to make it all lovey-dovey or anything like that. Just say that you like her and ask her if she's free to go out one evening.'

'I'm not sure,' Michael said softly.

'Of course you are,' Gavin argued. He opened his bag and took out his large

14

writing pad and a pen. 'Come on, Michael. It could be your last chance.'

He placed the writing paper and the pen on the table in front of his friend.

'But I don't even know how to start,' protested Michael.

Gavin put the pen into Michael's hand. 'How about, 'Dear Shireen . . . '?' he said.

2

Alison and Shireen decided to walk to school rather than to take the bus. Even at eight-fifteen in the morning, the day promised to be yet another scorcher. As they approached the gates, Shireen checked to see if Michael was around. He was often on early morning prefect duty, stopping the lower-school pupils from taking the short cut across the teachers' car park.

'We're too early,' grumbled Alison. 'He won't be here until half-past.'

Shireen smiled. 'We should've walked slower.'

They headed for their form room, intent on gathering up the books they needed for the day, before returning to the school gates and making their entrance for a second time.

'We've got to make it look as though we've just got off the bus, though,' suggested Alison as she scooped up her maths folder and her chemistry textbook from inside her desk. 'Mind you, even if

16

we came face to face with him, you'd probably go all shy again and run away.'

Shireen was silent, gazing into her desk at the neatly folded square of white paper with her name on it.

'What's up?' asked Alison.

Shireen opened the letter and stared wide-eyed at the signature on the bottom of the page, before reading its contents.

'What is it?' asked Alison, impatiently.

Shireen silently handed her the note.

Alison read what Michael had written and squealed with delight. 'I don't believe it!' she gasped. 'He wants a date.'

'What do I do?' asked Shireen, nervously.

Alison sighed. 'What do you mean, 'What do I do?'? You say 'yes' of course. You arrange to meet him somewhere.' She grabbed her general notebook and sat at her desk. 'Come on,' she said, 'let's write him a reply.'

★   ★   ★

'You can't come this way!' yelled Michael at the girl who was approaching from the gym block and crossing towards the out-of-bounds car park.

Gavin grabbed the sleeve of Michael's white shirt. 'It's that Alison,' he said. 'That friend of Shireen's.'

Michael gulped. 'Do you think she's found the letter already?'

Gavin grinned. 'Looks like it.'

Alison, acting ultra-cool, came right up to them. 'I know I shouldn't be coming this way,' she said, staring into Michael's bright blue eyes. 'But I'm only being a messenger.'

She handed him a folded note, smiled at him, winked at the open-mouthed Gavin . . . turned and nonchalantly walked on towards the school's year-eleven entrance.

'What's it say?' Gavin asked excitedly.

Michael opened the note. 'I bet she's not interested,' he said, softly.

He read what Shireen had written:

Meet me outside the technology block after school.

'Well?' asked Gavin.

Michael smiled. 'So far, so good.'

* * *

Shireen stood at the side of the technology block, trembling. She'd laughed loudly when, earlier, Alison had asked if she should accompany her. Now she wished that she'd said yes.

Michael left Gavin in the cloakroom and crossed the playground towards the technology block; his heart pounding and his mouth becoming drier and drier by the minute. Gavin had told him exactly what to say . . . and now he was rehearsing the lines over and over again as he slowly approached the beautiful blonde girl in the distance.

As he reached her, he smiled . . . and said nothing, fearful that the carefully planned words would just come out as one long croak.

She smiled back and spoke. 'Hi!'

'Hi!' he said. 'You turned up then?' It was a stupid thing to say, and he knew it.

'It looks like it, doesn't it?' she replied, sounding just as awkward as him.

He put out his hand. 'I'm Michael.' What *was* he saying?

She laughed and took his hand, shaking it formally. 'I know,' she said. 'You're Michael and I'm Shireen.' She knew that she'd have to take control immediately. His palm was running with sweat and she noted the nerve in his cheek which gave an involuntary twitch. He was obviously even

19

more nervous than her.

'I have to catch the eighty-one bus,' she said. 'Do you want to walk me to the bus stop?'

She immediately began to worry that Alison might still be there, at the stop, waiting.

'A good idea,' he said. 'I have to go that way home, anyway.'

They walked across the school play-ground towards the main gate, keeping an arm's length distance between them, desperately seeking things to say, both hoping that they weren't boring each other with mundane tales about school life and their transport home . . . and the gloriously warm weather.

From the top of the road, Shireen saw the familiar figure of Alison, leaning against the bus stop, her bag at her feet. Michael saw her too.

'There's your friend,' he said. 'Are you travelling home with her?'

Shireen knew that if she stopped at the bus stop and began talking to Alison, that would be *it*! He'd say his goodbyes, walk on . . . and the opportunity would be lost for ever. She grabbed at her only chance.

'Actually, I don't live very far away,' she

blurted out. 'I'm down on The Belling Estate. I could walk it from here.'

His heart began to race even faster. 'I could walk you right home if you like,' he suggested. 'It's on my way,' he lied, hoping that she wasn't aware that he lived in the opposite direction.

'That would be nice,' she said. 'We don't have to pass the bus stop,' she added quickly. 'We can cut through The Grove.'

Alison lifted her head when she heard the bus approach. At the top of the road, she saw Michael and Shireen cross at the roundabout and walk on past the post office into The Grove.

* * *

By the time they'd reached Shireen's front door, the subject matter of their conversation had moved on to their likes and dislikes, their favourite bands . . . and what both of them did in their spare time.

'You could come in for a tea or coffee or something if you want,' Shireen said, surprising herself at her boldness.

'Great,' said Michael.

He followed her down the hall and into the large kitchen at the back of the house.

'No one home?' he asked. He wished he hadn't said that. He wasn't meaning to imply that he was glad that they were alone together. 'It's not that . . . '

She smiled at him as she began to reach for the kettle. 'Mum'll be home from work soon,' she said. 'No. There's no one in.'

She filled the kettle under the kitchen tap.

'So you're leaving school at the end of term,' he said.

'Yes,' she replied. 'How do you know?'

He shrugged. 'Oh . . . people talk. A friend of mine told me. My friend, Gavin.'

'The tall boy with the ginger hair?' She took down two mugs from the rack and placed some coffee in each of them.

'Yes. He's my best mate. He told me . . . ' He hesitated. 'He told me that if I didn't ask you out soon, then it'd be too late.' There! He'd said it!

She faltered as she screwed back the lid on the coffee jar. Her fingertips felt numb; her mouth was dry.

'That would be nice,' she stammered. 'Where shall we go?'

She blushed.

He blushed too. 'I don't know. I . . . '

They heard the key turn in the front

22

door. 'It's only me!' called a voice.

'My mum,' Shireen said to Michael.

'Should I go?' he asked.

She panicked. She didn't want him to leave. 'Why?' she asked.

Shireen's mother entered the kitchen and was surprised to see the handsome boy being entertained by her daughter.

'This is Michael, Mum,' said Shireen.

Mum nodded. 'Hello, Michael.'

'He's in year twelve, doing his A-levels,' she said quickly.

Mum began to remove her coat. 'Wise boy. Can't you persuade my daughter to stay on and do *hers*?' she smiled.

Shireen tutted. 'I'm going to college,' she informed Michael. 'I want to be a children's nurse. It's what I've always wanted to do. Doing A-levels would just be a waste of another year.'

'At least she's got a nice, long summer break before she starts, haven't you, Shireen?' Mum said.

Shireen glared at her, warning, 'Mum!'

Mum sighed. 'All right. All right.' She turned to Michael. 'Her father wanted us all to go away for the summer. The south of France. We used to go camping there every year until Shireen suddenly decided that camping was a little unsophisticated for her.'

Shireen laughed. 'It wasn't that at all, Michael,' she explained. 'I just felt that, what with starting college in September, I'd be better off spending my time here, seeing friends and things.'

'*I'm* going away,' Michael said suddenly.

Shireen's heart skipped a beat. 'Really?' she said, trying not to sound too concerned. 'Where?'

'Spain,' he said. 'I'm doing Spanish as one of my A-levels, so I'm spending the summer there.'

'The whole summer?' asked Shireen, dreading his reply.

'Yes. I'm off in three weeks and I don't get back until September.'

'That'll be fun,' said Shireen, forcing a smile.

Mum saw the far-away look in her daughter's eyes. 'Kettle's boiling, Shireen,' she said.

★ ★ ★

'Are you sure you don't want to stay for something to eat?' asked Shireen as she saw Michael to the front door.

24

'No. I'd better be off,' he replied. 'Mum'll be cooking something for me.'

She felt desperate, as he began to walk down the path towards the road. He hadn't repeated the offer of taking her out. She wondered if he'd changed his mind.

He turned at the gate and came back. 'So, are we going out then?' he asked.

She beamed. 'When?'

'Do you like Decoy?'

'They're not my favourite group,' she laughed. 'But yes . . . they're all right.'

'They're playing at The Granville tomorrow night,' he said. 'Have you ever been?'

She'd been once, when Alison had insisted they'd go . . . and she hadn't liked it at all. It was dark and smoky and loud. Certainly not her sort of club.

'Yes, I have,' she replied.

'Do you like it?'

'Yes. It's great,' she said.

'Tomorrow night then?'

'Great.'

'I'll pick you up about eight. All right?'

'OK.' She laughed. 'I'll see you tomorrow at school, anyway.'

'No you won't,' he replied. 'I'm not going in tomorrow. I haven't got any lessons. And I can do my private study better at home.'

She was disappointed. School would be very dull, knowing that he wasn't somewhere in the building.

'See you, then,' he said.

'See you.'

He kissed her quickly on the cheek; a shy, furtive peck. And as he strolled off along the path, she closed the door and waited a few seconds, composing herself before returning to the kitchen to be greeted by knowing looks and a broad grin from her mother.

★ ★ ★

As soon as he'd turned the corner, Michael ran like the wind; through The Belling Estate, past The Oval Shopping Centre and across the park to Gavin's house. He stood panting at Gavin's front door, having hammered loudly three times on the brass knocker.

Gavin opened the door and gasped. 'You're sweating like a pig,' he said. 'And you're as red as a beetroot.'

'Can I come in?' Michael asked urgently. 'I've got a problem. I mean

26

. . . *we've* got a problem.'

Both boys climbed the stairs to Gavin's bedroom, littered as usual with CDs and textbooks and writing paper.

'So, how did you get on?' asked Gavin. He sat on his bed and began to chew on a half-eaten chocolate bar which he'd thrown down when he'd heard Michael's frantic knocking.

Michael sat beside him. 'She's fantastic,' he said. He laughed. 'I'm so in love!'

Gavin grinned. 'Oh sure. Love, is it? Already?'

'No, honest, Gav, she's really nice.'

'Apart from being stunningly beautiful, of course.'

'Of course,' said Michael.

'So, did you actually *speak*?' asked Gavin.

'Yes. We talked a lot,' Michael informed him. 'I know everything about her.'

Gavin looked at his watch. 'In an hour and a half, eh? And you know everything?'

'And I've asked her out,' Michael said, confidently.

'Good on yer!' laughed Gavin. 'Well done, mate!' He slapped Michael's knee. 'I was beginning to think you didn't have it in you.'

'Well, I've proved you wrong, haven't I?' Michael said, proudly.

'So when are you going out together?'

Michael fell silent.

'Michael?'

'That's the problem, Gavin.'

'Not tomorrow night?'

'Yes, 'fraid so.'

'But we've arranged to go to The Granville to see Decoy,' sighed Gavin. 'You and me. I've got the tickets, Michael.'

'I know. And that's the other problem I've got,' Michael said, softly. 'I told Shireen I'd take *her* there. I'm sorry. It just sort of came out. I don't know why I said it. I just couldn't think of anything else.'

'But you haven't got a ticket for her,' said Gavin. 'And they've probably sold out by now.'

'Well . . . ' Michael hardly dared ask. 'I was wondering . . . ?'

'Oh no!' said Gavin, firmly. 'Definitely not. You're not having my ticket, Michael. No way!'

3

They arrived at The Granville in Gavin's battered, purple Mini, parked in a side street and raced to the foyer of the club to enquire if there were still any tickets left for the following evening.

'It depends how many you want,' said the woman in the booking office. 'We've only got three.'

'We only need one,' said a relieved Michael as he took out his wallet.

'We'll have two,' Gavin jumped in. He grinned at Michael. 'I'm not playing gooseberry to you two. I'll have to bring someone . . . and you can pay for them.'

Michael reluctantly paid for the two tickets, kept one for himself and handed the other to a beaming Gavin.

'So who are you going to ask?' he said.

Gavin shrugged. 'I don't know. Perhaps I should ask Shireen's friend, Alison. Then we could go as a foursome.'

Michael was delighted. 'Hey, that's great, Gavin. We'll have a laugh.'

As they headed back towards the Mini, Gavin was beginning to look serious. 'I hope she won't get any ideas, though,' he said. 'I don't want her thinking I fancy her, or anything like that.'

'She's very attractive, Gavin,' said Michael. 'And she winked at you, don't forget.' He paused. 'She seems to be quite a 'fun' person.'

★ ★ ★

By lunchtime the following day, a heavy storm had prevented the upper school from sunbathing on the amphitheatre steps.

'Not that it matters,' Shireen said dreamily, as she and Alison lounged in their form room, half reading, half gazing out at the rain bouncing off the windows. 'It wouldn't be the same walking down the steps, knowing he wasn't there.'

'You've really got it bad, haven't you?' smiled Alison. 'I only hope he's not a let-down tonight. I can't believe you're going to The Granville with him. You *hate* The Granville. You swore you'd never go there again.'

'I might get to like it,' grinned Shireen,

'if I've got hunky Michael with his arm around me.'

Gavin popped his head into the year-eleven common room, saw the two girls and crossed to them. 'Hi!' He dragged up a spare chair and sat opposite.

Shireen and Alison were surprised to see him. 'Hi!' they replied in unison.

'We haven't really spoken, have we?' he said. 'I'm Gavin. But I'm sure you know that, already.'

Shireen smiled at him. 'We *had* heard. Yes.'

'So . . . I hear you're going to The Granville tonight with Michael,' he said to Shireen.

'That's right,' Shireen replied.

'She can't wait,' interrupted Alison. 'She loves The Granville, don't you, Shireen?'

Gavin didn't look at Alison. 'Do you?' he asked Shireen. 'I do too. I've had loads of good times there.'

'It'll be packed tonight,' added Alison.

Gavin still didn't look at Alison. He was suddenly struck by Shireen's dark green eyes. She and Michael would certainly make a handsome couple. 'I'm going too,' he said. 'I really like Decoy.'

Alison couldn't contain herself. '*You're*

31

going? Not with Shireen and Michael, surely?'

Shireen nudged her friend with her elbow. 'Alison!' she reprimanded her. 'He didn't say he was going with us.'

'Oh, but I am,' said Gavin.

Shireen looked horrified. Her first date with Michael, and his best friend would be tagging along.

Still Gavin didn't address Alison. He looked down at his shoes, attempting, but failing, to appear non-chalant. 'I thought we could go as a foursome,' he said nervously. 'You know . . . you and Michael and me and Alison.'

'Really?' gasped Alison. 'Oh, that would be fantastic.'

'Er . . . yes,' stammered Shireen. 'That would be really nice, Gavin.'

'I'm picking Michael up at quarter to eight,' Gavin went on. 'And then we'll come and pick you two up at your place, Shireen. Is that all right?'

'Yes,' she said. 'Perfect.'

'Pick us up?' enquired Alison. 'You haven't got a car, have you?'

For the first time, Gavin glanced in Alison's direction. 'Of course I've got a car,' he replied. He stood and looked down at Shireen, 'So, see you tonight then,' he said. And he left.

'Well! What about that?' said Shireen. 'You've been asked out on a date, Alison.' She laughed. 'By the boy you've always called 'that tall one with the ginger hair'.'

'He's quite nice, though, isn't he?' said Alison. 'He's quite good-looking really, when you get close up to him. And he's got great legs.'

Shireen laughed. 'Great legs? *Long* legs, you mean.'

'*And* he's got a car,' sighed Alison. 'I've always wanted to go out with someone who's got a car.'

'Aah . . . ' Shireen said, tongue in cheek, ' . . . that's why you've suddenly decided he's quite nice. It's the car!'

Alison giggled. 'Of course it's not the car. It's *him*. I *like* him.' She grabbed Shireen's arm. 'Hey! I hope it's a car with plenty of *leg* room.' She shrieked with laughter. 'I hope it's not a Mini!'

★　★　★

'You look really gorgeous,' Alison said as she and Shireen sat side by side, staring

33

into Shireen's bedroom mirror while applying the last of their make-up.

'You too,' replied Shireen. 'I think I prefer your hair up like that.'

'I hope *he* does,' grinned Alison. 'You don't think he's taking me along out of sympathy, do you?' she asked. 'You don't think he felt sorry for me, because I was being left out?'

'Don't be ridiculous,' replied Shireen. 'Anyway,' she added, 'would that bother you? You want to see Decoy. That's the whole point of the evening. It's not as though you fancy him or anything, is it?'

Alison smiled at her through the mirror. 'Well . . . '

Shireen's eyes widened. 'You *do*! You *do* fancy him!'

A car-horn sounded from the street outside and Alison raced to the window to take a look. She stared open-mouthed and then turned back to Shireen, with a glint in her eye. 'They're here,' she said. 'In the *Mini*!'

★ ★ ★

The Granville was, as expected, packed. Michael managed to grab a table in one of the crowded, dimly-lit alcoves and all four sat, looking out across the empty dance-floor.

'Not a lot of elbow room, is there?' Gavin shouted above the DJ's over-amplified sound.

'It'll get better when people start dancing,' Alison replied, knowledgeably. 'We'll probably have this alcove all to ourselves then. It's early yet.'

'What time are Decoy on?' asked Shireen.

Michael looked at his watch. 'Not for ages. Shall I get us some drinks?'

They placed their orders and, as Michael squeezed through the crowd to get to the bar, Gavin turned to Alison. 'Do you want to dance?' he asked her.

Alison hesitated, not wanting to leave Shireen sitting on her own. 'Shall we wait till Michael gets back?' she said. 'Anyway, I hate being the first on the dance-floor. I'll feel a bit braver when there are more people up there.'

He smiled at her. 'Yeah. Let's wait for Michael. We'll all dance together, eh?'

Alison stared at him, examining his features: the spiky red hair, the strong Romanic nose, and the broad jaw just

35

beginning to sprout a layer of reddish-blond whiskers. Although he was far from being conventionally good-looking, he was, to Alison's mind . . . extremely attractive. She was aware, however, that this date with him might be just a one-off; that he'd probably only asked her along to make up a foursome.

Michael eventually managed to struggle back through the crowd and place the ordered drinks on the table in front of his companions.

'It wasn't too bad, actually,' he said. 'I thought I'd be ages, but there's a lot of bar staff.'

Building up towards Decoy's imminent arrival, the DJ decided to play their latest hit single, which still sat at number five in the charts. The raucous sound of *Get up And Dance* reverberated off the club's walls and, almost as one, the crowd surged towards the dance-floor, responding to the lead singer's demand.

'Shall we?' asked Michael, smiling at Shireen.

'Why not?' She put down her drink and followed him on to the dance-floor.

Without speaking Gavin put his hand out to grip Alison's.

She stood. 'I feel braver *now*,' she giggled . . . and she pulled him to his feet.

★ ★ ★

When Decoy hit the stage, a little after eleven, the floor was crowded and the alcoves totally empty. The musicians lived up to their reputation of being one of the best of the new 'live' bands and the crowd yelled and screamed for encore after encore.

Alison had got completely wound up in the excitement, leaping up and down with the other revellers, all shoulder to shoulder, hemmed in around the stage. Gavin leapt up and down beside her, occasionally giving her a wide grin as they both sang along to Decoy's last top-forty hit.

Shireen kept looking at her watch, knowing that she'd promised her parents she'd be home by midnight.

'Michael,' she said finally. 'I really must go. If you want to stay, then Alison and I can get the bus.'

'Don't be daft,' he said. 'Of course you're not getting the bus.' He pushed his way towards the stage and tapped a sweating Gavin on the shoulder, mouthing, 'We're off. Are you coming?'

Gavin looked disappointed, but grabbed Alison's hand and pulled her through the crowd to where Shireen stood, still eyeing her watch.

'Sorry,' said Shireen. 'But my mum'll panic if I'm not home soon.'

Gavin smiled at the beautiful, blonde girl whom Michael had his arm wrapped around. 'No problem,' he said. 'Let's go.'

As they left the club, the air hit them like a wet sponge, making their sweat-streaked faces feel cold and clammy.

'It was so hot in there,' gasped Shireen. 'You'd have thought they'd have air-conditioning . . . especially during a hot summer like this.'

'Not so hot tonight,' said Gavin as he began to cross the main road. 'I think it's all changed after that storm.'

'Too hot for an arm around you?' Michael whispered to Shireen.

'Not too hot for *that*,' she whispered back.

As Alison followed Gavin across the road, Michael put both his arms around Shireen's waist and pulled her towards him. They stood at the kerb, staring into each others' eyes.

'Have you had a good evening?' he asked her.

'Great, thank you. Have you?'

'I really like your company, Shireen,' he said.

'Good,' she smiled. 'I'm glad. I like being with you too, Michael.'

'So can we do it again?' he asked, a little tentatively.

'When?' she asked. She laughed, realizing she was sounding more than keen.

'I'll see you at lunchtime tomorrow,' he said. 'On the amphitheatre steps. And we'll arrange something, eh?'

'Supposing it's raining tomorrow?' she asked.

'Who cares about a bit of rain,' he replied. 'If you're there it'll be sunshine all the way.'

They both laughed at the comment.

'You should be a poet,' she said. 'Or *not*.'

He grinned. 'Yeah. Writing crass comments on greetings cards.'

They stopped laughing and stared, silently, at each other. He tightened his grip around her waist and pulled her even closer. Then, gently . . . very gently

. . . he kissed her.

'Shireen!' Alison called from the other side of the road. 'I thought you were worried about getting home?'

★ ★ ★

Gavin huffed and puffed as he tried over and over again to start the motor.

'What's wrong with it?' he said. 'It's never done this before!'

Alison sat in the front passenger seat, staring out through the windscreen. 'Perhaps it's damp,' she suggested. 'After the storm.'

'Don't be stupid!' he snapped. 'It got us here, didn't it?'

Alison was furious. 'Don't talk to me like that, you great pillock! I was only trying to help!'

Gavin was ashamed at his outburst. 'Sorry,' he said. 'I didn't mean to sound . . . '

Michael leant forward from the rear seat, his hand still holding on to Shireen's. 'I thought you were supposed to know all about cars, Gavin,' he said.

Shireen looked at her watch. 'I'm going to be ever so late,' she said. She too leaned forward. 'Look, I'm sorry, Gavin, but I'm going to have to get the bus.'

'Leave the car here, Gavin,' suggested Michael. 'We'll come back for it tomorrow.'

'I can't leave it here,' sighed Gavin. 'It won't have any wheels left by the morning. You know what they're like around here.' He turned to face Shireen and Michael. 'I'm sorry about this,' he said. 'It's ruined the evening.'

'Of course it hasn't,' Michael assured him. 'It's not your fault.'

'You can never trust old bangers like these,' added Alison, insensitively.

'You lot had better get the bus,' said Gavin. 'I'll ring my dad and get him to come over. He'll sort it out. I'll see you all at school tomorrow.'

★ ★ ★

Alison had never before felt so unwelcome, even though Michael and Shireen had engaged her in conversation throughout the bus journey home. She tried to avert her eyes every time Michael squeezed Shireen's hand a little more tightly. She knew they wanted to be alone,

41

but the rest of the bus was full. There was nowhere else to sit, except on one of the long seats . . . facing them. The walk home from the bus stop to The Belling Estate was even worse. It seemed endless to Alison as the two new love-birds strolled along, arm in arm beside her.

Finally, they reached Shireen's gate.

'I'll see you tomorrow,' Alison said quickly as she began to walk off.

Shireen stopped her. 'Alison! You're not going home on your own. Michael'll walk with you.' She smiled at him. 'Won't you, Michael?'

He tried to cover his disappointment. He wanted a few more minutes alone with her. He was hoping for a goodnight kiss. And so was she. But she also knew that her father was probably watching her every move from the landing window.

'Of course I'll walk you home, Alison,' he said.

He quickly kissed Shireen on the cheek. 'See you tomorrow,' he said. 'Come rain or shine.'

Then he walked off across The Belling Estate with Alison.

4

Alison strolled slowly past the tennis courts and down towards the amphitheatre. She knew that she wouldn't be welcomed by Shireen and Michael, but she couldn't think what else to do.

She reached the top of the steps and saw her best friend, lying on her front. Michael lay beside her, with his arm around her. They were both engrossed in conversation. For a while she stood and stared at them. Then she turned and walked back into school . . . heading for the library.

'It's a sort of 'exchange',' Michael tried to explain. 'This guy from Spain will come over and live in my house. And I'll be living with his parents in Madrid. It should be fun.'

'Do you think so?' asked Shireen. 'I wasn't that keen on Spain myself. I prefer France.'

'Except when you're camping,' he laughed.

'Not keen on camping. No.' She laughed too.

'You've probably only seen the Costas in Spain, though, haven't you?'

'Yes. Two weeks in Marbella.'

'Me too,' he informed her. 'But this time I shall see the *real* Spain. No English or German tourists. Just Spaniards. It's the best way to study the language.'

'I wish *I* could speak a foreign language,' she sighed. 'I've never been very good at it.'

'If you came with me you'd be speaking fluent Spanish in no time,' he said.

She felt her heart flutter.

'Not that you could of course,' he added, quickly. 'I don't think that the Spanish family in Madrid would approve if I turned up with you in tow.'

'I don't suppose they would,' she replied softly.

He gently ran his fingers upwards . . . along the nape of her neck and then through the back of her blonde hair. 'But it's a nice thought, isn't it?' he said.

'Very,' she purred. She lifted her head to face him. 'It's a pity you have to go away for so long,' she said, plaintively. 'Five weeks.'

'Yes,' he replied. 'I was really looking forward to it, but now I'm not so sure.'

'Why's that?' she asked, although she understood exactly what he was implying.

'I think you know why,' he said as he teasingly approached her lips with his.

She closed her eyes and turned over, wrapping her arms around his broad back. And as he kissed her, she saw images of sun-drenched Spanish beaches and palm trees. She could almost feel the incoming tide gently lapping over their sand-and-salt-streaked bodies. And she wished, so much, that she could go with him.

* * *

He arrived at eight o'clock as arranged and found her ready to leave.

'Don't keep her out too late, Michael,' Shireen's mum demanded. 'I know it's Saturday tomorrow, but it's still a twelve o'clock deadline, don't forget.'

'Of course I won't,' he replied, fully aware that he was charming Shireen's mum with his dazzling white smile. 'We're only going into town for a walk. We'll be back well before midnight. I promise.'

As they opened the front door, they

were surprised to see Alison standing there, about to ring the bell. She was holding a carrier bag.

'Oh. Sorry,' said Alison, feeling extremely embarrassed. 'I didn't know you two were going out tonight. I just thought I'd bring round these CDs before I . . . '

Shireen too was embarrassed. She didn't want to let Alison down. They'd always gone out together on Friday evenings, ever since either of them could remember. 'Didn't I tell you, Alison? I thought I said that Michael was calling for me tonight.'

Alison began to blush. 'Yes, but I didn't think he'd be here quite so early, so . . . '

'We're only going for a walk,' said Shireen. 'You can come with us if you like.'

It was only a half-hearted gesture as all three of them were aware.

'Don't be silly,' said Alison. 'Anyway, I'm supposed to be meeting someone later,' she added as she handed Shireen the carrier bag. 'It's just that I had an hour to spare and so . . . ' She turned to walk away, calling back over her shoulder, 'I'll see you in school on Monday.'

'I'll ring you in the morning,' Shireen

called after her. 'We'll arrange something for tomorrow night.'

'OK!' Alison replied and she raced off before her blushes became more obvious.

★　★　★

The park, on this long, hot summer's evening, was still open and Michael led Shireen by the hand, along the gravel path towards the pond. They sat on the wooden bench, watching the ducks being fed by an old woman carrying a crumpled paper bag filled with bread.

'Who do you think she's meeting?' asked Michael.

'Who? That old lady?' asked Shireen.

Michael laughed. 'No. Alison. She said she was meeting someone later.'

'No one,' Shireen assured him. 'She just said that, because she was embarrassed.' She sighed. 'I do feel awful about it. We always go out together on Friday nights.'

Michael put his arm around her and pulled her close to his side. She rested her head on his shoulder.

'You should've told me,' he said. 'You can't go letting her down like that. She *is* your best friend, Shireen. We could've

47

gone out tomorrow instead.'

Shireen sighed. 'Yes. You're right. I hate the thought of hurting her.'

Michael smiled. 'Hey, you don't think she's meeting Gavin, do you?'

'If only,' replied Shireen.

'Does she like him?' asked Michael.

'Yes. She says she finds him attractive. What about *him*?' she enquired. 'Does *he* like *her*?'

Michael shrugged. 'He said he didn't fancy her,' he replied. 'But that was before we all went to The Granville.' He pulled Shireen closer to him. 'They seemed to get on all right together, didn't they?'

'But hasn't he said anything about her?' she asked.

Michael felt guilty. He'd been so full of his own new-found romance with Shireen, he hadn't even asked Gavin about Alison. 'Er . . . no,' he said. 'No, he hasn't mentioned her. Perhaps I should ask him how he feels about her.'

Shireen smiled. 'Yes. Perhaps you should.'

★ ★ ★

Earlier, having left Michael and Shireen canoodling away their lunchtime on the amphitheatre steps, Alison had gone to the library to write some letters. She was hoping to get a job to see her through the summer holidays, but so far none of the letters she'd written had received a reply. However, she was determined to keep trying. She wasn't surprised to find the library almost empty. It was such a beautiful day and she knew that anyone with any sense would be spending their lunchtime outside.

The only other person there, sitting at the long table near the door, nose in a book on car-mechanics, was Gavin. At first she wondered if she should quietly disappear. She didn't want him to think that she was following him; that she was coming on too strong. Then she decided that she had every right to be here and if he didn't like the thought of her sitting with him, then he could always make some excuse and leave.

She deliberately sat right opposite him and took out her note-pad and pen. He didn't look up. He stared down at page 106, headlined: THE OIL FILTER. His hands covered his ears, blocking out any sound around him. He was totally engrossed. Alison grinned mischievously. She picked up her pen and began to write:

Dear Gavin,

This is not a love letter! I'm sitting opposite you now, staring at your ruggedly handsome face and wishing I could run my fingers through that beautiful red hair. This is not a love letter! I can just see those little gingery blondish hairs peeping up over the top of your open-necked shirt and thinking how nice it would be if you looked up at me at this very moment with those sparkling brown eyes. This is not a love letter! As our two best friends seem to be totally in lerv (!) and not able to spend time with us any more, I thought we could maybe go out together somewhere. There! I bet you've never had an invitation like that from someone as beautiful as me. Take up the offer, or live to regret it!

Love, Alison. xxx
PS This is not a love letter.
PPS You've got lovely legs.

Fighting back the giggles, Alison pushed the letter across the table towards Gavin's textbook.

He didn't see it.

She pushed it further.

He still didn't react.

She sighed, picked up the letter and placed it down on top of page 106: THE OIL FILTER.

Gavin stiffened and stared at the handwritten page in front of him. Without looking up, he slowly read the letter. Alison watched the corners of his mouth turn up as he tried to suppress his laughter. Then, still not looking at her, he grappled in the top pocket of his jacket which was hanging over the back of his chair, and took out a pen. He turned over Alison's letter and wrote on the back of it:

Dear admirer,

Thank you for your letter. I'm glad you like my handsome face and red hair. And yes . . . you're right . . . my legs are rather nice. Let's meet tonight at eight-thirty outside McDonald's.
From, Gavin.
PS This is not a love letter!

Still not looking at her, he pushed the letter back across the table.

Alison picked it up, read it, packed her bag and began to leave the library. As she passed by the back of his chair, she playfully ran her hand over his hair. Just one stroke . . . and she was gone.

★   ★   ★

'Do you fancy a burger or something?' Michael asked Shireen as they walked, hand in hand, through the town centre. 'I've got some cash on me.'

They reached McDonald's and Shireen sat on a low wall outside the restaurant, which surrounded a tiny shrub-bed recently planted by the local council.

'I'll wait here,' she said. 'It's too nice to sit indoors.'

As Michael left her to queue at the counter, Shireen gazed up at the cloudless sky, just beginning to darken. She could see the crescent moon and the promise of a thousand stars which would soon appear. It was a glorious night, a gentle breeze now weakening the stifling heat of the day and, for the first time, it really hit her that in just a few weeks' time, Michael could be staring up at this very moon and these very same stars, although he'd be a thousand miles away.

Her feelings began to frighten her. She knew it couldn't be love. Not yet. Hadn't her mother told her, many times, that love takes time to grow; that there was no such thing as love at first sight. And Shireen realized that she didn't *know* Michael at all. There was so much to learn about him but, unfortunately, they didn't have time to spare. Soon he'd be leaving and when he returned, things would be so different. She'd be about to start college and he'd be returning to Melthorn High.

From that moment, she determined to make the most of the next few weeks; to find out if he really was the boy she hoped he was . . . and if he was . . . then a five-week absence shouldn't make any difference to the way they felt about each other. Five weeks! Her stomach lurched. How would she bear it?

She gazed through the restaurant window and saw him slowly easing forward in the queue, his blond hair appearing almost white in the bright lights above him. And then her eye caught the diners on the corner table and she gasped, audibly. She could hardly believe it. Gavin and Alison, chatting away to each other, smiling, laughing over their burgers and fries. She stood and raced into the restaurant, tugging at Michael's arm and pointing in Gavin and Alison's direction.

Michael smiled broadly. 'Well, well, well,' he said. 'Would you believe it. There's *my* best friend . . . with *your* best friend. Dating. Secretly.'

Shireen crossed to their table and sat. They both looked at her, rather nervously.

Shireen smiled. 'You didn't tell me you two were out on a date tonight.'

'We're not,' Alison replied quickly. 'We're just friends,' she added, sounding peculiarly guilty. 'It's not a date. Not a *real* date. Is it, Gavin?'

His reply surprised her. 'Course it's a real date. Why?' he asked her, with a mischievous grin. 'Are you ashamed to be seen with me or something?'

Alison laughed. 'No. It's just . . . '

Gavin reached forward and took Alison's hand. 'We're going off to The Granville later,' he informed Shireen.

'Are we?' asked a shocked Alison. 'You didn't say.'

'You two can come with us if you want

to,' added Gavin.

'I can't,' replied Shireen. 'I've promised to be back before twelve and you know what Friday nights are like at The Granville. Nothing gets started till eleven-thirty.'

Michael arrived at the table with a tray of burgers, fries and coffee. 'Hi, you two!' he said. 'What a surprise.'

'Gavin and Alison want us to go off to The Granville with them,' Shireen told him, 'but I can't.'

'Oh. Shame,' said Michael. 'Who's on tonight?'

'It doesn't stop *you* going, Michael,' Shireen said.

Michael gripped her hand. 'And why should I want to go without you?'

'Are *we* still going?' Alison asked Gavin, trying to sound cool, trying to pretend it didn't really bother her if they went or not.

Gavin looked at her in surprise. 'Of course we are. Don't you want to?'

'Yes. Yes, course I do,' stammered Alison. 'But it's just the two of us and . . .'

'Have you finished stuffing your face?' Gavin interrupted her.

55

Alison laughed. 'Yes.'

'Then let's go,' he said as he reached out for her hand.

He and Alison stood.

'What are you two doing tomorrow?' Gavin asked Michael and Shireen.

They looked at him, blankly.

'Nothing,' said Michael.

'Nothing. Why?' Shireen added.

'So how about a picnic in the country? The four of us. I can take us in the car.'

'In that Mini?' gasped Alison. 'Are you sure?'

'That would be great,' said Michael.

'Fantastic,' added Shireen.

'Right!' Gavin grinned. 'If you all bring some eats and drinks, I'll pick you up at Shireen's about ten.'

'Are we really going in that Mini?' asked Alison, her eyes twinkling. She looked at Shireen and grinned. 'Not a lot of leg room, is there?'

Gavin smiled. 'I hope you're not referring to *my* legs,' he said. 'I thought you really liked my legs, Alison.' He kissed her on the cheek, which surprised everybody, including Alison. Then he turned to Michael and Shireen,

56

announcing in a mock whisper, 'Alison really likes my legs.'

Alison blushed as Gavin led her to the door, leaving their stunned friends gazing after them.

5

'I think it was down here somewhere,' announced Gavin as he carefully manoeuvred the battered Mini along a pot-holed country lane. 'Mind you, I haven't been here since I was about five years old, so I might've got it wrong.'

Alison bumped up and down in the seat beside him. 'Five years old!' she groaned. 'Gavin! You'll never remember where it is! Anyway, I still can't understand why we're going to somewhere called Bluebell Wood,' she added. 'There's not going to be many bluebells about in July.'

'There won't be *any*,' said Shireen from the back seat. Sweat was trickling down her face and she leaned forward trying to get some air from Alison's open window.

Gavin tutted. 'It's not called Bluebell Wood,' he explained. 'We called it Bluebell Wood when we were kids.'

'That's because it was full of bluebells, I expect,' said Michael, somewhat sarcastically.

'That's right,' replied Gavin. 'We used

to come here in the spring.' He looked through his mirror and saw Michael and Shireen's sweat-streaked faces. 'I'm sorry,' he said. 'Perhaps this wasn't a good idea after all. I wasn't expecting it to be *quite* so hot today.'

'It's not your fault, Gavin,' said Michael. 'It's a great idea. It's just that we're a bit cramped.'

Even though they were all wearing just shorts and T-shirts, they'd spent more than two hours in extreme discomfort. And although Gavin had made such an effort to please, being squeezed into his tin can of a car on such a hot, sticky day, had made them all feel a little bit irritable.

Gavin suddenly skidded the car to a halt. A white signpost pointed the ways to Skegly and to Chatsfield.

'I think it's Skegly we want,' he said. 'But then, I might be wrong. It could be Chatsfield.'

'Chatsfield sounds nicer,' smiled Alison. 'Let's go to Chatsfield.'

Gavin took the right fork, heading for Skegly.

'Or, of course, we could always go to Skegly,' giggled Alison.

The lane began to narrow, winding its

way through the vibrant yellow fields of rape, before rising upwards past picture-book green fields scattered with poppies and unidentifiable wild flowers.

Alison sighed and clutched Gavin's bare knee. 'Better than the park, Gavin,' she said.

Shireen agreed. 'It's beautiful, Gavin. Bluebells or no bluebells.'

Gavin suddenly shrieked like a small boy, 'This is it! I'm sure this is it.' He stopped the car at the side of a crumbling stile, leapt out . . . and gazed open-mouthed across the sheep-dotted field beyond. 'This brings back memories,' he sighed.

The others tumbled out after him, gasping for air, their clothes sticking to them.

'It's over there,' explained Gavin. 'On the other side of this field. Bluebell Wood.'

'Without bluebells,' grinned Alison.

'We can't just leave the car here,' said Michael. 'Nothing can get by.'

'If I remember right, there's a lay-by further up the hill,' said Gavin. 'Let's unload the picnic and you lot can wait here while I go and park up.'

Armed with carrier bags, they crossed the field and headed for the trees on the other side. It was a relief to be in the shade, though the wood was not as inviting as they'd all hoped. The hurricane of 1987 had flattened much of it . . . and the fallen trunks, some thankfully sprouting signs of new life, had blocked the way through to where Gavin, as a small boy, used to picnic with his parents.

'What a shame,' he said as they climbed over fallen oaks and beeches, brushing aside clinging ivy and other creepers. 'It's been totally destroyed.'

'And not a bluebell in sight,' said Alison, trying to lighten Gavin's disappointment.

They struggled onwards, encouraged by Gavin's calls from ahead, until the wood finally came to an end and opened out on to rolling green hills, littered with the yellows and whites of a thousand butter-cups and daisies.

The sun, now a little watery, felt extremely pleasant and they quickly found a spot where they could settle, fling off their shoes and spread out their picnic on the white sheet which Shireen had borrowed from her mother's airing cupboard.

As the others began to eat, Michael took off his shirt and lay on his stomach, feeling the warm rays settling between his shoulder blades. The gold chain around his neck glinted in the sunlight and Shireen leaned over and gently fingered it. 'I haven't seen this before,' she said. 'Is it new?'

Michael immediately sat up and helped himself to a sandwich. 'Yes. Do you like it?' he asked.

'I've got one almost the same,' she replied. 'See?' She pulled out the chain, hidden under her blouse.

Michael didn't look at it. There was no need to. He'd seen it when they'd been lying on the amphitheatre steps together. And that's when the idea had struck him.

'Michael?' she asked, wondering why he hadn't responded.

'I know,' he said, dismissively, as he reached out for a can of Coke. 'They're very similar.'

Alison suddenly gasped. On the far side of the field, she could see something moving towards them. She raised her hand, shielding her eyes from the sun, and tried to make out the approaching mass.

'Gavin? What's that?' she asked.

Gavin stared and laughed. 'Cows,' he said. 'They're coming to find out what we're doing.'

They all turned to look.

'I hope you're right, Gavin,' said Shireen. 'I hope they're not bulls.'

'They're bullocks,' said Michael. 'They won't hurt you. They're just curious.'

The herd slowly approached and stopped a few metres away, gazing at the picnickers.

Alison froze. 'I don't like it,' she said. 'They look as though they're going to charge.'

'I hope they don't charge much,' said Gavin. 'I've only got fifty pence on me.'

The others laughed.

Gavin flung his arms around Alison's neck. 'They won't hurt you while I'm around,' he said with a smile. 'Because I'm brave . . . and I'm strong . . . and I'm . . . ' He suddenly whisked everything off the white sheet and stood, holding it up like a matador's cloak towards the staring herd. '*Olé!*' he yelled, as he stamped his feet and twirled around with the cloth, flapping it up and down. 'Come on, you wild beasts! Do your worst!'

Michael stared at him, incredulously. 'He'll never grow up,' he said with a smile.

'You'll get a shock if one of them *did* actually charge,' said Shireen.

The bullocks, looking bored, slowly began to turn and amble away.

'There!' laughed Gavin. 'They know who's boss around here.'

'Perhaps you ought to give Michael a lesson in bullfighting,' suggested Alison. 'He may need it in Spain if he comes across any of those wild, black bulls over there.'

Shireen suddenly looked glum. She'd managed for a few hours to push the fact aside that Michael would soon be leaving. Alison saw the look on her face and rather than draw attention to it, she quickly tried to change the subject. 'So what about this after-lunch surprise you've got for us, Gavin?' she said. 'What is it?'

He playfully grabbed her around the neck again and dragged her backwards until she was lying flat out on the grass. She screamed and giggled.

'If I told you, then it wouldn't be a surprise, would it?' he said. He leaned across her, pinning her arms by her side ... and then quickly kissed her, before releasing her. 'Was that surprise enough for you?' he asked.

She sat up, laughing. 'Call that a surprise?' she said, pretending to wipe away his kiss on the back of her hand. 'I hope it's a bit better than that.'

★ ★ ★

Having packed up the picnic things into their carrier bags, they continued the walk across the field, heading for what Gavin called his big surprise. The sun had now regained its full power and Michael had put his T-shirt back on. He wanted his body to retain its golden tan. He didn't want to burn and peel.

A short trek through another tiny wood brought them out on to a cliff-edge and they all beamed when they saw the sea ahead of them.

'I had no idea we were this close to the coast,' said Shireen.

'That's why I asked you not to look at the map,' Gavin informed them. 'This is the surprise. An after-lunch swim.'

A steep dirt-path led them down, through banks of nettles, bustling with butterflies, to a tiny shingle beach.

'We used to come here in the spring,' said Gavin, 'But it was too cold to swim. I don't think anyone else knows it exists.'

'It's fantastic,' sighed Shireen as she gazed longingly at the tiny waves lapping gently on to the shore. 'What a pity we haven't brought our swimming things.'

'Who needs them!' yelped Michael as he kicked off his trainers, peeled off his T-shirt and raced to the water's edge. Gavin did the same, chasing after him.

'You'll get your shorts wet!' called Alison as she watched them run straight into the sea.

'They'll dry again!' Gavin called back.

Alison looked at Shireen and smiled. Shireen returned the smile. Then, dropping the carrier bags on to the shingle, both girls raced down to the sea and, fully clothed, they leapt into the water.

★ ★ ★

Exhausted though content, they lay back on the shingle, feeling their wet clothes quickly being dried out by the sun. Shireen, fearful of getting burnt on this sun-trap of a beach, used one corner of the picnic sheet to lay across her face as a protective shield. Michael lay beside her, one arm wrapped around her, wishing they could stay like this for ever. Further along the beach they could hear Alison's squeals of delight as she and Gavin searched the rock pools for tiny crabs and shrimp.

'I had a letter today,' Michael mumbled, his face down in the shingle.

Shireen removed the sheet from her face. 'Oh?'

'From Spain.'

'Oh.' She sighed. 'From the family you're staying with?'

'Sort of. Actually, it's from their son. My exchange partner.'

'Really? Does he sound OK?' she asked.

'Yes. He sounds quite nice,' Michael said. He too sighed. 'He sent a photo.'

'And?'

'Frightened me a bit,' he said. 'He's extremely good-looking.'

Shireen sat up, looking down at Michael. He turned over on to his back and gazed up at her. 'He looks like a film star.'

'What, like Michael Caine, do you mean?' she laughed.

'More like Brad Pitt,' he replied, grimacing.

'So, what's the problem?' she asked. 'You won't even meet him, will you?'

'Briefly,' he said. 'In Madrid. You'll meet him here.'

'Me? Why should *I* meet him?' She was surprised.

'Because I was hoping you'd look after him, maybe. Take him around and show him some typically English places. Would you?'

'Of course I will. If you want me to,' she replied.

He grinned up at her. 'I *did* want you to. But now I've seen his picture, I'm not so sure.'

'You sound jealous,' she said.

'I would be,' he replied. 'If I thought you'd fancy him.'

She gently ran her finger across his forehead. 'That dark Mediterranean look doesn't appeal to me,' she replied, honestly. 'I go for blonds.'

'He *is* extremely handsome, Shireen.'

'He couldn't possibly be as handsome as you, Michael,' she said.

He reached up and pushed her hair away from her eyes. Then he slowly pulled her down towards him. She lay her head on his chest, listening to the beating of his heart, gently stroking up and down his side with her fingertips.

'Look what we've found!' yelled Alison from above them. They felt her shadow fall across them, blocking out the sun. Michael and Shireen sat up, trying not to show their irritation at being disturbed. Gavin stood beside Alison, holding out his hand.

'It's a gold cross!' said Alison, excitedly. 'From a chain. Someone must've lost it when they went swimming.'

'I thought you said no one else comes here, Gavin?' asked Michael.

Gavin shrugged. 'Perhaps it got washed up from another beach.'

'Maybe it was lost on a beach abroad somewhere,' suggested Shireen. 'It could've been washed here from France.' She grinned. 'Australia even. Who knows?'

'Or Spain,' Gavin said, without thinking. 'You could take it over with you when you go, Michael . . . and ask around. See if it belongs to anyone.'

He laughed loudly. 'Here,' he said as he handed it to Michael.

Michael refused to take it. 'You found

it,' he said. 'You keep it.'

Gavin insisted. 'I haven't got a chain to put it on,' he said. 'Put it on *yours*,' he added. 'Then when you're away it'll remind you of the day we all spent here.'

Michael silently took the cross. 'Thanks, Gavin,' he said, somewhat sadly. 'I will.'

★   ★   ★

They sat on the stile, carrier bags at their feet, looking back across the sheep-inhabited field, waiting for Gavin to bring the car from the lay-by.

'What a fantastic day it's been,' sighed Shireen.

'And it didn't really matter about the bluebells, did it?' laughed Alison.

Michael looked along the road and saw Gavin strolling forlornly towards them. 'Oh, dear,' he said. 'Something's wrong.'

'Oh no,' said Alison. 'Don't say he can't start the car.'

She looked at her watch. It was six o'clock. 'My parents were expecting me home for tea. I'm late as it is!'

Gavin reached them and sighed, resignedly. 'Sorry,' he said. 'I can't start the car.'

6

With the Mini's bonnet propped open by a gnarled old stick, Gavin unsuccessfully fiddled around with the engine until he had oil up to his elbows. The others stood around the car impatiently, hoping that he'd soon find the fault and that they could all set off for home.

'I'd help if I could,' said Michael. 'But I know nothing about cars, Gavin. I'm sorry.'

Alison looked at her watch and tutted. 'My dad'll go mad,' she said. 'I should've borrowed his mobile as he suggested. Then at least he'd know where we are.'

Gavin looked up, helplessly, from the engine. 'It's no good,' he sighed. 'I can't see what's wrong with it.'

'Could it be the oil filter?' Alison asked, haughtily.

'I think we ought to try to get to a phone-box,' said Shireen. 'We can call the AA or something, can't we?'

Gavin shrugged. 'I'm not a member.'

'What about your dad?' suggested

Michael. 'He'll come and help, surely.'

Gavin climbed back into the Mini, picked up an oily rag and began to wipe his hands. 'Alison and I will go and see if we can find a phone-box,' he said. He looked up at Michael and Shireen from the car's opened door. 'You two may as well stay here. It's pointless us all going.' He leapt out from the car and put his hand out to take Alison's. 'Come on,' he said.

Alison backed away from him, grimacing at his oil-stained fingers. 'I'll come with you,' she said with a half-smile, 'but I'm not holding that filthy hand.'

Gavin held up both his palms to show her just how ingrained the oil was. Then he began to approach her, with a mischievous grin.

'You dare,' she warned him as she started to run backwards.

He suddenly leapt towards her, reaching out for her hair with his fingers. Alison screamed and then giggled as she turned and began to run along the country lane away from him. Gavin chased after her, whooping and yelling. Michael and Shireen watched the pair until they became two laughing and screaming dots in the distance.

'He'll never grow up,' said Michael as he took Shireen's arm.

'And neither will she,' smiled Shireen. 'They're well matched.'

They strolled back to the stile and Michael climbed over it. Shireen followed him, carrier bag in hand.

'We may as well make ourselves comfortable,' he said. 'They could be hours.' He took the bag from Shireen and reached inside it for the white sheet, which he spread out on the grass, carefully smoothing away all the wrinkles. Then he lay on his back and gently pulled Shireen down beside him. She lay, silently, her arm across his chest, listening to his low breathing.

'Comfy?' he whispered.

'Very,' she replied. She cuddled up close and shut her eyes, feeling the warmth of the late afternoon sun on her cheeks.

For minutes they said nothing, though both their heads were teeming with thoughts. She wondered if he would be able to read her mind; those thoughts and dreams of hers being so graphic. He hoped *she* couldn't read *his*.

Finally he spoke, keeping his eyes

closed, not turning to her. 'Have you done this a lot?'

She too kept her eyes closed, responding softly, 'Done what?'

'Lain like this?' He hardly dare ask. 'Beside someone? Like this?'

'No,' she replied, honestly.

'But you've been out with other people?'

'Of course,' she said. 'Quite a few times. But not like this. I've never *felt* like this.'

He was silent.

'What about you?' she asked.

'Me?'

'Have you ever been this close to someone?' She was sure of the answer. Someone like *him*? Someone as good-looking as *him*? Of course he'd lain like this before, beside other girls. Many of them. As close as this. Closer than this. She was sure.

'No,' he said. 'Never.'

She opened her eyes and looked at his tightly shut lids, examining their blond lashes and the bronzed, broad brow above them, slightly furrowed in consternation.

'Never?'

'Never.'

'But you've had loads of girlfriends?'

'No.'

74

'Of course you have,' she said. 'You must've been out with lots of girls.'

'I've never been out with anyone,' he said, worried that his naïvety might put her off him completely.

'Really?' She was amazed.

He opened his eyes and turned his head to look at her. 'Really.'

'But you must have had girls throwing themselves at you,' she said.

He grinned, shyly. 'What's that got to do with it?' he asked.

She leaned up on one elbow, staring at him in disbelief. 'Are you saying that I'm the first person you've ever been out with?'

'Yes.' He gulped, turned his head away from her and closed his eyes again. 'Does that worry you?'

She put her head on his chest and sighed, 'Not at all.'

'So you'll have to be gentle with me,' he smiled.

She too smiled. 'I'll be *very* gentle with you, Michael.'

'With my heart, I mean,' he added. 'Don't break it, will you?'

She sighed deeply, though she felt there was no need for a reply.

'Night-night,' he said softly.

She giggled. 'Night-night.'

★ ★ ★

Alison and Gavin had walked for miles, trying to find a call-box; Alison constantly looking up at the sky, watching the light gradually fading.

'It'll be dark soon, Gavin,' she said, fearfully. 'Suppose we can't find our way back to the car? We've got to find a phone soon.'

Gavin too was worried, but his reply came out as irritation. 'What do you want me to do? Conjure up a call-box from thin air?'

Alison smiled up at him, childlike. 'You could *try*,' she pleaded, softly. 'For *me*.'

He laughed. 'Right,' he said. 'Here goes.' He closed his eyes and pretended to wish. Then he opened them. 'Done it!' he said with a grin. 'For *you*.'

As they turned the next corner and passed the sign for Chatsfield, Alison's mouth dropped open. A call-box was just ahead of them.

'How did you do that?' she asked.

He put his arm around her. 'Magic,' he replied.

* * *

Michael deftly unclipped his gold chain and removed it. He threaded it through the loop on the small cross which Gavin had given him and held it up for Shireen to see.

'It looks really good,' she said. 'Here,' she took the chain and placed it around Michael's neck, refastening the catch.

'A gold cross,' said Michael. 'Should go down well in a Catholic country like Spain.'

Shireen stood and crossed to the stile. 'It's getting cold.' She shivered.

'And dark,' added Michael. 'Any sign of them?' he asked as he pushed the cross and chain inside his T-shirt.

Shireen looked along the country lane for Alison and Gavin. 'No.'

'They've been gone for ages,' said Michael. 'I hope they haven't got lost. Surely they've found a phone-box by now?' He stood and gathered up the sheet, pushing it into the carrier bag. 'Perhaps we should go and sit in the car. It'll be warmer.'

'There they are!' Shireen suddenly yelled. Far off, in the gloom, she could see two tiny figures approaching. She leapt over the stile and ran along the lane towards them. 'Where have you been?' she yelled.

Alison laughed. 'If we'd had to walk any further we'd have been home! There would've been no need to find a phone.'

'But you did find one?' Shireen asked, hopefully.

'Yes,' said Alison. 'And I've rung your mum too, so she knows exactly what's going on.'

'And my dad's on his way with his pick-up truck,' added Gavin. 'But it'll probably take him a couple of hours.'

As they reached the stile, Michael was leaning nonchalantly against it. 'What kept you?' he asked, coolly. 'I thought you'd deserted us for good.'

'Michael suggested we sit in the car,' said Shireen. 'It's getting chilly.'

Gavin grinned. 'I've got a better idea. Let's get some sticks together before it gets dark.'

'What? And build a fire?' asked Alison

with childlike excitement in her eyes.

Shireen sneered at the idea. 'And rub two sticks together to light it, I suppose?'

'Don't be daft,' laughed Gavin. 'I've got a box of matches in the car.'

★　★　★

'I'm starving,' said Alison, as the four of them sat around the tiny fire which was spitting and crackling under the moonlit sky. 'I suppose it's because bonfires remind me of baked potatoes.'

They all looked at her quizzically.

'Dad always cooked baked potatoes in the bonfire on fireworks night,' she explained. 'The thought of it made me feel hungry.'

Gavin put his arm around her. 'I'm hungry too,' he grinned. 'Hungry for love.'

She giggled and pushed him away, affectionately. 'You could go and catch one of those sheep, Gavin,' she said. 'We could have roast lamb.'

'Or one of those bullocks,' added Michael. 'A nice rump steak.'

'I'm not going anywhere,' said Gavin. 'I'm staying here . . . with my love.' He laughed and once again wrapped his arm around Alison. This time she didn't push him away.

'It *is* sort of romantic, isn't it?' sighed Shireen as she placed her hand on Michael's leg. 'Sitting under the stars, around a camp-fire. I wasn't expecting to be doing anything like this today.' A chill ran down her spine. 'I don't suppose we'll ever do this again.'

Michael gripped her hand. 'Of course we will,' he said, softly. 'When I get back from Spain, the first thing we'll do is come back here and build a fire. Just like this.'

'Let's make it a pact,' said Gavin seriously. 'We'll all come back here to celebrate your return home.'

'But it'll be autumn by then,' said Alison, thoughtlessly spoiling the dream. 'It'll be cold and wet. It won't be like this.'

The others fell silent.

'Have I said something wrong?' asked Alison.

'No, you're right,' agreed Shireen. 'Everything will have changed by then. Winter'll be coming on. I'll be at college and you lot will still be at school. It'll never be the same again.'

'Then we ought to make the most of it *now*,' said Michael. He gently ran his fingers through Shireen's hair before leaning forward and kissing her. She responded to his kiss, wrapping her arms around him and running her fingers up and down his back.

'Well?' Alison asked Gavin. 'Follow my leader?'

Gavin laughed. 'Follow my leader!' he replied as he gripped Alison tightly in his arms and kissed her.

And as the fire crackled and burned more brightly, shooting tiny sparks towards the star-littered sky, the two couples, lost in their euphoria, were unaware of the pick-up truck slowly heading along the lane towards them.

7

Alison arrived early at school to find Shireen in the North Cloakroom, staring forlornly through the domed window towards the main gates.

'So, the big day's arrived then,' said Alison. 'I thought it'd never get here.'

It was the last day of term. The end of Shireen's school life. And it felt even worse than she could possibly have imagined. Not only was she going to leave all her friends behind her; she now had to face the fact that she was going to be separated from Michael. They'd had such a short time together and just when everything seemed to be perfect, they were about to be torn apart. Even the weather had decided to be unkind on their last day together. After weeks of glorious sunshine, today it was drizzling, which meant they wouldn't be able to spend their last lunchtime on the steps of the amphitheatre.

'Hasn't he come yet?' asked Alison as she watched the early arrivals ambling through the gates. 'I'd have thought he'd have been here really early today. After all, you haven't got long together, have you?'

Shireen felt the lump tightening in her throat; the knot of sadness which was preventing her from replying to Alison's questions.

Alison noted the pained expression on her best friend's face and she gently placed an arm around her shoulder. 'He'll be here soon,' she said. 'Don't panic.'

A group of year-eleven school-leavers suddenly raced through the gates, whooping loudly. Some of them couldn't wait to say their goodbyes and Alison wondered if there'd be the usual after-school hurling of flour bombs and eggs which, during yesterday's main assembly, the Head had strictly forbidden.

'There you are,' said a voice from behind them. Alison turned to see Gavin grinning at them. 'We've been here for ages,' he said. 'I thought we'd arranged to meet in the common room.'

'Is Michael here?' asked Shireen.

'Yes,' replied Gavin. 'He's getting a bit worried, wondering why you haven't turned up.'

Shireen smiled. 'Thanks.' She immediately headed towards the common room.

Alison began to follow her, but Gavin quickly grabbed her arm. 'Where are you going?' he asked.

'Don't you want to go to the common room, too?' she asked, surprised.

Gavin winked at her and took her hand, leading her towards the library. 'Let's leave them on their own for a while, eh?'

Alison immediately realized how insensitive she'd been. 'Oh, yes. Of course,' she smiled.

'It's not going to be easy for them today,' explained Gavin. 'He's off to Spain this evening and who knows what'll happen after that?'

'He'll be back in five weeks,' said Alison. 'It's not long.' She paused, thinking on what she'd just said. 'No. It *is* long,' she added. 'I wouldn't like it if *you* were going away for five weeks.'

'And let's face it,' said Gavin, seriously, 'he may decide he likes it out there. He might meet someone else and decide to stay.'

'He can't,' replied Alison. 'He's coming back to take his exams.'

Gavin shrugged. 'All I'm saying is, you

never know. They've got to make the most of today.'

They walked into the library and both of them automatically sat at the table where they'd first passed notes to each other.

'Anyway, here's the good news,' grinned Alison. 'I've got a summer job.'

She expected Gavin to react favourably. He didn't.

'Oh!' he said, glumly. 'What sort of job?'

'McDonald's,' she informed him.

'Oh.'

'I really need it, Gavin,' she said. 'I haven't any money at all. I thought you'd be pleased for me.'

'I'm just being selfish,' he said softly. 'I was looking forward to spending the holiday with you. I wanted to go to the coast and things.'

'I'll have some days off,' she said quickly. 'And I'm not working every evening.'

He reached out for her hand and forced a smile. 'Well, that's all right, then.'

★ ★ ★

Michael was careful how he answered Shireen's question.

'Well, yes, I *am* looking forward to it. I've always wanted to go to Spain. But I'm all mixed up inside.'

'Me too,' she said.

'I'll write every day,' he promised. He paused. 'I wish you were coming with me.'

Her eyes filled with tears and she bit hard on her lip. 'How would you get any studying done, if I was there?' she said. 'You've got to speak Spanish all the time. That's why you're going. If we were both there, we'd be chatting away in English.'

'Yes. I know you're right,' he said. 'It's just so . . . '

'As long as you don't spend all your time talking to some beautiful Spanish girl,' she said, trying to smile through her tears.

'And talking of beautiful Spanish people,' grinned Michael, 'look at this.' He reached into his bag for an envelope which he handed to Shireen.

She opened it and took out a photo.

'Is this him?' she asked. 'The Spanish boy?'

'Pedro. Yes. Well? What do you think?'

She studied the picture. The boy was

extremely handsome, as Michael had said, with a strong jaw and huge dark eyes topped by long black lashes. His hair, cut very short, was jet-black and his smile dazzled through his tanned skin.

'Isn't he ugly?' laughed Shireen.

'You can see why I was worried, can't you?' said Michael.

'What have you got to worry about?' she asked seriously, as she put the photo back into the envelope. 'Yes. He's very handsome. But not as handsome as you.'

'Really?'

She leaned forward and kissed him. 'Really. There's no one else for me, Michael. There couldn't be. I love you.'

These were the words he was waiting for; the words he was hoping she'd say on their last day together. He stood and raised her from her chair, wrapping his arms around her and pulling her tightly towards him.

'I love you too, Shireen,' he said. 'I really do.'

★　★　★

By lunchtime, the drizzle had turned to heavy rain and Shireen was sorely

87

disappointed. Had she realized yesterday, that what she'd believed to be her *penultimate* lunchtime on the amphitheatre steps with Michael, would, in truth, turn out to be her *last*, then she would have relished the time even more. But, through a sudden change in the weather, it suddenly occurred to her that she'd already spent her last day on the steps, lying beside him, their arms wrapped around each other. It would never . . . *could* never, happen again. Not there! Not on the steps.

'Don't be daft,' said Alison as she and Shireen entered the Central Hall to join the dozens of school-leavers all autographing each others' shirts and blouses. 'Of course you won't be cuddling up to him on the steps again, but does it really matter *where* you do it?'

'No, I suppose not,' replied Shireen. 'It's just full of great memories, that's all. It's where it all started.'

'Then you'll have to keep those memories in your head,' Alison wisely lectured her. 'You'll never forget those days on the steps . . . just as I'll never forget the library.'

'The library?' Shireen was curious.

Alison laughed. 'Never mind.' She took out her pen. 'Here, let me be the first to sign your blouse.'

Gavin and Michael waited at the top of the Central Hall stairs, not wishing to get involved with the tearful girls and the *seemingly* cheerful boys, who'd all suddenly realized that their school days were over. This was it!

'I'm going to really miss her, Gavin,' Michael said, flatly. 'I don't know how I'm going to cope when the time comes to say goodbye.'

'Is she going to the airport with you?' asked Gavin.

'Yes. Unfortunately.'

'Don't you want her to?' questioned a surprised Gavin.

'I *did* want her to,' Michael explained. 'It was my suggestion. My parents are working late, so they won't be there. And I thought it would be really great for us to spend a couple of hours together before I leave. But now, I'm not so sure it's a good idea. It's going to be very difficult.'

'Alison and I can come too, if you want,' said Gavin. 'Then Shireen won't be left alone when you pass through the boarding gate.'

'*Would* you?' asked Michael.

Gavin smiled. 'I'm sure you'd do the same for me.'

'Look after her for me while I'm away,' added Michael. 'Don't let her be lonely, will you?'

'Alison and I'll keep our beady eyes on her,' said Gavin. 'Don't you worry about that.'

Beaming, Shireen ran up the steps towards the boys, followed by a giggling Alison.

'Look at the state of *her*!' exclaimed Alison.

Shireen's white blouse was covered in signatures, the biggest of which, in green ink, was Alison's.

Shireen handed a pen to Gavin. 'Your turn,' she said.

Gavin signed his name on a white space on Shireen's shoulder. 'Treasure this,' he laughed. 'I might be famous one day and this'll be worth a fortune.'

Alison grinned and tutted. 'Famous for *what*?'

Shireen handed the pen to Michael.

'I'm not signing it,' said Michael, firmly.

Shireen looked disappointed. 'Why?'

'Because all these signatures are from

people you'll drift away from. Eventually. Most of them, you'll never see again after today. But as we're going to spend the rest of our lives together . . . '

Alison looked at Gavin. 'Aaah! Why can't you say romantic things like that?' she asked with a twinkle in her eye.

'Because I'm not as wet as him,' grinned Gavin. 'I'm a *real* man.'

Michael laughed. 'Are you sure?'

Alison giggled. 'Shall I tell you what he said to me yesterday? Bless him.'

Gavin began to blush. 'You dare!' he said.

Alison shrieked with laughter and took his hand. 'Come on, lover boy,' she said. 'Let's go for a walk in the rain and leave these two alone.'

★ ★ ★

'But I can't come to the airport, Gavin,' said Alison, in despair. She stood in the puddle-filled playground, looking down at her feet. 'I've got my training session at McDonald's tonight.'

Gavin was shocked. 'I didn't think you'd be starting straight away.'

'I'm sorry,' said Alison. 'You'll have to

go on your own. I can meet you both afterwards. About ten?'

Gavin shook his head. 'The flight isn't till nine-thirty. We won't be back here till gone eleven.'

'Well, what can I do?' asked Alison. 'I can't take time off, can I? It's my first evening. If I say I've got to go early, I'll be sacked before I've even started.'

Gavin shrugged. 'Don't worry. I'll look after her. I'm quite good at comforting maidens in distress.'

Alison looked a little concerned. 'Just so long as you don't comfort her too much,' she said.

Gavin was annoyed, and hurt, at the suggestion. 'What's that supposed to mean?'

'Nothing,' Alison replied softly. 'Sorry. That was stupid of me.'

'Yes. It was,' Gavin said, harshly. 'Michael asked me . . . us . . . to look after her. And if you're not there . . . '

'I said I'm sorry,' said Alison. She grabbed Gavin's hand. 'Please. Don't let's argue. Not today.'

★   ★   ★

92

'I'll go and wait in the coffee shop,' said Gavin as he stood with Michael and Shireen at the gate to the departure lounge. He shook Michael's hand. 'Have a great time, mate,' he said. 'And don't do anything I wouldn't do.'

Michael affectionately slapped him on the back. 'I'll see you in five weeks, Gavin. Look after her, eh?'

'Trust me,' replied Gavin, with a grin. 'Come and find me in the coffee shop when you're ready, Shireen,' he added. And he left.

Michael clutched Shireen tighter than he'd ever done. 'I don't want to go,' he said. 'All the excitement has disappeared. I just want to stay here with you.'

She put her hand into her coat pocket and pulled out a small, purple envelope. 'Here,' she said. 'I've written to you already and you haven't left the ground yet.' She smiled. 'It's the first of many. Hopefully.'

He took the envelope and put it into his pocket. 'A love letter?' he grinned.

'Might be,' she said. 'Might not.'

'I should've written you one, shouldn't I?' he said.

'Haven't you?' she asked, not at all

surprised that he hadn't.

'Might have,' he said. 'Might not.'

They kissed. And both felt the tingle that surged through their bodies, now entwined as one.

'If I'm going to go, then I'd better go now,' he said. 'If I linger any longer, I might just change my mind.'

She was determined not to cry. She wanted to look good for him as he turned to wave his last goodbye. No tears. No ugliness. She smiled. 'I'll miss you,' she said.

'I love you, Shireen,' he replied and he picked up his hand luggage and walked towards passport control.

She waited for him to turn back at the gate. He didn't. He couldn't. He didn't want her to see him looking so distressed. He walked swiftly through the gate and disappeared from view.

Shireen gave one involuntary sob. She now knew what people meant by 'a breaking heart'. Hers was aching. A dull pain in her chest, like no other she'd ever felt. It's only five weeks, she thought. Only five weeks. Five weeks? Five long, painful weeks. She turned and headed for the coffee shop, where Gavin was waiting. And there she fell into his opened arms, laying her head on his shirt and bursting into the tears which had been promising to flow for hours.

'Oh, Gavin,' she sobbed. 'I can't bear it.'

He gently stroked her hair. 'He'll be back before you realize he's gone,' he said, trying his best to comfort her. He took out a brown envelope from his pocket and handed it to her. 'He told me to give you this,' he said.

She stared at it. 'What is it?'

He smiled. 'How should *I* know? A love letter, probably.'

She quickly tore open the envelope and took out the letter and the rest of its contents. The message on the letter was simple. 'This'll keep me close to you.' She then picked up the gold chain with the tiny cross on it and opened the catch.

'Will you put it on for me?' she asked, as she turned her back on Gavin.

He put the chain around her neck and fastened it securely.

★　★　★

As Gavin and Shireen silently made their way home from the airport, Alison struggled to make sense of the McDonald's till, although her mind kept drifting away from the task in hand. She could think of nothing more than the stupid quarrel between her and Gavin and although she regretted making such a crass comment, she felt that his reaction was a little over the top. And she wondered how he and Shireen were coping together at the airport. Without her. And she was very angry with herself for even contemplating the thought that perhaps . . .

★ ★ ★

Michael waited until he could see the lights of Crawley beneath him, before opening the purple envelope and taking out the gold chain which Shireen had enclosed. He smiled. Great minds think alike. He put the chain around his neck and fingered it gently. Then he read the love letter which had accompanied it.

8

Alison looked across at the clock on the mantelpiece. It was almost eleven and she was hoping that Gavin would call her to say that he and Shireen were back from the airport and that Michael was safely on his way to Spain.

She gazed back at the TV screen, oblivious to the programme being transmitted. Her parents had already gone to bed, asking her to keep the volume low as they had an early start the following day. Alison knew that the phone would disturb them if it rang, but still she willed it to do so.

There was a strange feeling welling up inside her; the fear that now that Michael had left, things wouldn't be the same between her and Gavin. They wouldn't be able to spend so much time together . . . alone. Now that Michael was away, they had to look after Shireen. They couldn't just leave her on her own. Wherever they went, whatever they did, they'd have to ask Shireen to accompany them.

And Alison felt so guilty, that after all these years of friendship, she was now considering Shireen to be an intrusion into her new-found relationship with Gavin. But she liked Gavin . . . *really* liked him. And she felt angry that Michael had had to leave and spoil everything. She stared at the phone again and heard herself saying out loud, 'Please ring.'

Gavin had taken Shireen to her door and had left immediately, hurrying to the nearest phone-box. He'd picked up the receiver and was about to call Alison, but then, noting the time and realizing that her parents might be upset if he rang so late, he'd decided to leave the call until the morning. Anyway, it was possible that Alison had already gone to bed. She'd be tired after her first evening at work and he didn't want to annoy her by waking her up.

★ ★ ★

Michael was greeted warmly by his Spanish hosts as soon as he passed through passport control at Madrid's airport. Antonio and Suzana, in their late thirties, were elegantly dressed and Michael felt scruffy and a little uneasy in his denim jacket and jeans as he followed them towards the airport car park. Antonio walked ahead, pushing the trolley piled high with Michael's luggage, while Suzana spoke to her new house-guest in perfect English.

'I thought Pedro would be with you,' said Michael in faltering Spanish. He was tired and the words weren't flowing as he'd hoped they would. But then, it was the first time he'd put his study into practice.

'He's at home, packing his suitcase,' replied Suzana, with a smile. 'He flies to your home tomorrow lunchtime.'

Michael wiped the sweat from his brow. 'I hope he's packing plenty of sweaters,' he said, returning the smile. 'It's been very hot in England, but it probably won't last.'

'I know. I've been to London many times on business,' she said. 'And I've warned him that it's always raining there.' She laughed. 'We haven't seen any rain here for six weeks.'

As they approached the dark blue BMW, Michael checked his watch. It was midnight . . . and it was still so hot. He wondered what the weather would be like at twelve noon in Madrid. Then he realized he hadn't adjusted his watch to Spanish time. It was one o'clock in the morning here.

Antonio began to load the cases into the car's large boot. 'You must be tired, Michael,' he said. 'Don't worry. The drive is only thirty minutes.'

Michael tried to reply in Spanish. He couldn't.

Antonio grinned. 'English will do,' he said. 'You can settle in before you start trying the language.'

Suzana agreed. 'For the first few days we will speak English together, eh? Then we can change to Spanish, when you're ready, Michael.'

'And in the middle of the change over, we can mix it up a little,' laughed Antonio. 'A little bit of Spanglish!'

★ ★ ★

Shireen had gone to bed as soon as she'd arrived home. But there was no chance of her going straight to sleep. By the light from her bedside lamp, she read his note over and over again. Then she fingered the

100

tiny cross on the gold chain, hanging around her neck. She'd been looking forward to the summer holidays so much. A break before she started college. Long, sunny days when she and Alison could have some real fun, before that worrying transition from schoolgirl to college student. But this was before she'd become involved with Michael. And now she felt totally lost. Michael would be away for the whole of the summer . . . and Alison had a job. She would be alone for five weeks and she wondered how she would fill her days. And she wondered what Michael would be doing at this precise moment. Was he thinking of her, just as she was thinking of him?

She switched off the lamp and lay back, staring up at the ceiling, seeing only his face and that blond hair falling over his bright blue eyes. She could clearly picture his wide, white smile and the broad tanned chest adorned with the gold chain she'd given him. And she sighed deeply. She closed her eyes and turned on to her side, curling up into a tiny ball, like an infant in its cot. And she cried herself to sleep.

Bypassing the centre of Madrid, Antonio's BMW sped along the motorway to the outskirts of the capital. Michael gazed out of the rear window, watching the bright lights flashing by, feeling a little disappointed that his stay in Spain wasn't to be at the hub of Madrid. But then he realized that Pedro might also be thinking that he'd be staying close to the Houses of Parliament or Buckingham Palace. Pedro's stay in London would be in the suburbs, just as Michael's stay in Madrid would be in the outskirts.

Looking through his rear-view mirror, Antonio noted the look on Michael's face. 'It seems a long way out,' he said. 'But we have a metro not too far from the house.'

'It's probably better not to be in the centre,' lied Michael. 'I want to see how people in suburbia live.'

Suzana laughed. 'You mustn't call it suburbia here, Michael,' she informed him. 'The word 'suburbia' in Spanish means shanty town. And we certainly don't live in an old corrugated-iron hut.'

Michael smiled. 'Thanks for warning me,' he said.

Antonio left the motorway and sped through tree-lined streets to a modern four-storey block of apartments, where he parked the car in a underground car park and leapt out to retrieve the suitcases from the boot.

Pedro was waiting at the lift door as it opened on to the top floor . . . and Michael was immediately struck by the handsome features of his exchange partner. He looked even better in the flesh than in his photo.

'*Bien venido!* Welcome!' said Pedro as he vigorously shook Michael's hand.

Helping to carry the luggage into the apartment, Pedro babbled away in a mixture of Spanish and English, hardly able to contain his excitement about his visit to London.

'Let me show you my room,' said Pedro. '*Your* room, I mean,' he added. 'It is yours from tonight. I will sleep in another bedroom tonight.'

They passed through the huge, modern sitting room, incongruously bedecked with large paintings of what appeared to be old masters, and along the wide corridor towards the bedrooms.

'How many bedrooms are there?' asked

Michael. 'We have six,' replied Pedro. 'But one of them is used as a changing-room for the maids.'

'Maids?' Michael was astounded.

'We have two house assistants,' Pedro tried to explain. 'But they don't live with us. They arrive at seven o'clock to prepare breakfast and they will be here all day. So if you need anything . . . '

Michael stopped in his tracks and put down the bag he was carrying. 'Pedro,' he said, 'you do realize that we haven't anything so grand for you in England, don't you?'

Pedro turned to him and grinned. 'No maids?' he laughed.

'No,' said Michael, seriously.

Pedro winked at him. 'I think I can manage without maids,' he said.

They entered the large bedroom and Michael stared incredulously at the furnishings. Framed pop-art posters on every wall, an enormous bed — larger than king-sized — a TV, a huge hi-fi and speakers to match, shelves of books, CDs and videotapes . . . and an antique writing desk on which was placed the latest computer and printer.

'You also have your own bathroom,'

Pedro informed him. '*En suite*.'

Michael sighed. 'This is incredible!'

'You like it?' beamed Pedro.

'But in comparison to this, I'm afraid you're going to really slum it at my home,' said Michael.

'Slummit?' Pedro asked. 'What's slummit?'

Michael laughed. 'It doesn't matter, Pedro. I'm sure my family will make you feel welcome.'

'And now,' said Pedro, 'let's go and eat some supper. And then you can go to bed.'

★   ★   ★

As Michael ate a breakfast of fried eggs served to him by one of the maids, Shireen toyed with her piece of toast, wondering what she would do for the rest of the day. Her mother hurried into the kitchen, grabbed her bag and hurried out again. 'I'm off,' she called. 'See you tonight.'

Shireen was about to reply, when she heard the doorbell ring. She walked into the hall and saw the outline of a man's figure through the glass panelling of the street door.

Mum opened the door and stared at the

tall, ginger-haired boy on the step.

'It's OK, Mum,' said Shireen, from behind her. 'It's Gavin.' She called along the hall. 'Come in, Gavin.'

Mum passed the boy with a smile and hurried out to catch the bus to work.

Gavin closed the street door behind him and walked towards the kitchen.

'It's going to be another scorcher today,' he said.

'Great,' Shireen replied flatly. 'Do you want some breakfast?'

'A cup of coffee would be nice,' Gavin replied.

As Shireen reached for the kettle, Gavin sat and stared at her. 'How are you feeling?' he asked.

She forced a smile. 'OK, I suppose.'

'Really?'

'No, not really,' she replied. 'I feel pretty terrible, actually. As soon as I got up, it hit me. He's not here. And I don't know what to do with myself, Gavin. It feels so odd without him.'

'It must do,' said Gavin, sympathetically. 'I just thought I'd check on you. I knew you'd be a bit down.'

'Thanks for looking after me last night,' said Shireen. 'And I'm sorry I burdened you with my bawling.'

'No problem.' He stood. 'Here. I can make that,' he said as he reached for the coffee jar.

She handed him a teaspoon. 'Have you called Alison?' she asked.

'No. Not yet. I'll do it before she goes off to work.'

'She's working today, is she?' asked Shireen, surprised. 'I thought she was still training?'

'Doesn't take much training to work a McDonald's till,' grinned Gavin. 'Not for someone like Alison.'

'But she's not working every day, surely?' said Shireen. 'That's awful. You'll hardly see her.'

'That's what *I* said,' grimaced Gavin. 'But she needs the money. She's only doing certain shifts, though,' he added. 'Thank goodness. She's doing the lunchtime one today. So she'll be at home until about half-past eleven.'

'Well, why don't you call her from here?' Shireen suggested.

She picked up the phone and dialled.

★ ★ ★

'Shireen! How are you feeling?' asked Alison. 'I was going to call *you*, but I didn't think you'd be up yet.'

'I couldn't wait to get out of bed,' said Shireen. 'I was awake about four and I couldn't get back to sleep again.'

'Did he get off all right, last night?' she asked. 'Was the flight on time?'

'Yes. No problems.'

'So, what time did you get back?' she asked.

'Oh, I don't know,' replied Shireen. 'About eleven, I think.'

'I hope Gavin saw you home to the door,' said Alison.

'He did. He was so good, Alison,' she replied as she gave a beaming smile across the kitchen to Gavin. 'I'm afraid I was a bit wimpy. I had a really good cry. But he looked after me.'

'I'm glad to hear it,' said Alison.

'Do you want to speak to him?' asked Shireen.

The words hit Alison like a bolt of lightning. 'Is he there?'

'Yes.'

Alison tried to force a giggle. It wouldn't come out. 'He didn't stay there all night?'

Shireen laughed. 'Don't be daft. He's just got here. He came to see if I was all right.'

'Oh.'

'Have a word with him,' said Shireen as she was about to hand the phone across to Gavin.

'No!' said Alison. She automatically worried that she might have replied too harshly. She softened her voice. 'No. Tell him I'll see him later. He can come over here. Just give me half an hour to get ready.'

'Right.'

Alison hung up.

Shireen put down the phone. She was surprised and upset by Alison's comment. Of course Gavin hadn't been at the house all night. Surely she didn't think . . . ?

'Didn't she want to speak to me?' asked Gavin.

'I think she wanted to make herself look pretty for you, Gavin,' Shireen replied. 'Give her half an hour.'

Gavin smiled. 'She doesn't need half an hour to make up. She's beautiful enough.'

'Aah,' giggled Shireen. 'You really are fond of her, aren't you, Gavin?'

'Very,' he said, seriously. 'I just hope she

109

doesn't let me down.'

'Let you down? How do you mean?'

'You know,' he said, half stammering. 'Dump me for someone else. I don't think I could stand that.'

Shireen reached out and squeezed his hand. 'She won't do that, Gavin. She really likes you.'

'Do you think so? Honest?'

'Honest.'

Gavin poured the steaming water from the kettle on to the coffee granules. 'So, what are you going to do for the rest of the day?' he asked.

She shrugged. 'I've no idea. I'll probably write a letter.'

'To Spain?' He laughed. 'Already?'

'If it takes a week to get there,' she said, 'he'll be a whole seven days without hearing from me.' She laughed too. 'So that's my day taken up. A nice long love letter.' She thought. 'Don't know what I'll do tonight though.'

'We could go to the pictures tonight, if you like,' Gavin suggested. 'Me, you and Alison.'

'You don't want me hanging around with you,' she said, softly. 'I don't think Alison'll be very pleased if you tell her that

I'm going to accompany you on your date.'

'Alison won't mind,' said Gavin, assuredly. 'She loves your company.'

'Well, how about you ask her first?' said Shireen. 'If she's happy about the idea, then give me a call this afternoon.'

'Will do.'

'But if she's not keen, then I want to know. I'm not sitting there, playing gooseberry to you two . . . with Alison wishing I was a million miles away.'

'I'll call you,' he said. 'But I'm sure it'll be OK.'

★ ★ ★

'No, I don't mind,' said Alison. 'Of course I don't mind.'

She did mind, but she knew it would be churlish to say otherwise, especially when Shireen must be feeling so lonely. 'Give her a call, Gavin. Tell her I'll go round to her place when I've finished my afternoon stint. About seven. And you can pick us both up from there.'

9

Michael helped Pedro and his parents carry the luggage to the car. It was strange for Michael to think that in just a few hours Pedro would be sitting in *his* kitchen in England, sipping coffee from *his* mug and chatting with *his* mum and dad. And tonight he would be sleeping in *his* bed. He was concerned that Pedro, used to luxury, would be disappointed by his new surroundings. He was also a little worried that Pedro might take a shine to Shireen. No matter what she'd said about the photo, Michael had no doubts that when Shireen saw the handsome Spanish boy in the flesh, she would be bowled over.

As the last of the suitcases was packed into the boot, Michael handed Pedro a letter.

'You'll be seeing Shireen, Pedro,' he said. 'My girlfriend. Will you give her this for me?'

Pedro pocketed the sealed envelope. 'A love letter, eh?' He smiled. 'I make sure she gets it, Michael.'

Suzana looked at her watch. 'We're late,' she said not sounding the least bit hassled.

Pedro shook Michael's hand. 'Enjoy your stay,' he said. 'Everything that's mine is now yours.'

'And everything that's *mine* is yours,' Michael concurred. He paused for thought. 'Well . . . almost everything.'

Pedro wasn't sure what he meant. 'Enjoy España,' he said, as he climbed into the car.

Michael watched as Antonio reversed the BMW from its space and manoeuvred it from the underground car park into the street.

Dear Michael, she began.

This is ridiculous, I know, but I'm missing you so much already. I could hardly sleep last night, thinking about you and hoping that you settled in all right. I hope you're not living in some grotty little shack somewhere. It must be dreadfully lonely, living with a family of Spaniards and trying to communicate with them. Still, I expect the weather will be nice. It's a beautiful day here. Very hot and sunny again and Gavin has already been around this morning to see how I'm feeling. He suggested that I go to the pictures with him and Alison tonight, but I'm not sure about it. I don't want to get in their way. Anyway, Gavin will be ringing me later to say if it's OK or not. He's going to ask Alison. Oh, I do miss you . . .

She stopped writing when she heard the phone ring.

'It's me,' said Alison. 'How are you coping?'

'Fine,' lied Shireen. 'I thought you were going to work?'

'I'm off in about five minutes,' she replied. 'Gavin has just left. He was going to call you, but *I* decided to do it instead. Look,' she went on, 'you musn't worry about tagging on to us, Shireen. You're my best friend. You won't be in the way at all.'

'Are you sure? I wouldn't want to . . . '

'Don't be silly, Shireen,' Alison tried to convince her. 'I'm sure you and Michael would do the same for me if Gavin had to go away.'

'We would,' Shireen assured her.

'So, I'll be over to your place about

seven and Gavin will pick us up from there, OK?'

'In the Mini?' Shireen giggled.

Alison returned the giggle. 'I hope not. I've tried to persuade him that we'd be better off on the bus. But who knows?'

'Right. Thanks, Alison,' said Shireen, sincerely.

'See you tonight, then.'

'See you tonight.'

Alison put down the phone and began to head for the street door. She felt pleased with her good deed. There was no doubt that Shireen would be good company. She always was. The two of them had been inseparable for as long as she could remember. And she didn't see why her romance with Gavin should break up her greatest friendship.

* * *

Having been informed that he'd be left to his own devices for the day, Michael pondered on whether to take the metro into the centre of Madrid or to explore the area in which he was living. Antonio and Suzana had told him that they wouldn't be home until nine o'clock for supper, but as he had his own key, he was to do what ever suited him best. He decided to leave his exploration of Madrid until the following day. It would be better, he felt, to get used to his surroundings in this quiet, villagey kind of suburb. The noonday sun, however, had soon become almost unbearable as he'd strolled around ... even though he'd worn his baseball cap to keep the rays off his blond head.

Wandering through street after street of modern apartment blocks and detached houses fronted by gardens bedecked with purple bougainvillaea and scarlet hibiscus, Michael began to tire. He crossed a sleepy street and passed through a narrow lane where wild geraniums popped up their heads from the large cracks in the walls and pavements. It was a romantic kind of place in which to wander. The perfect spot to stroll arm in arm with someone you really cared for, cut off from the hustle and bustle of the modern world. And he was struck by the irony that Shireen would be sitting alone in her house while he wandered, solo, in the ideal setting for two young lovers.

★ ★ ★

Alison plunged into despair when she was asked if she would stay on to do the evening session at McDonald's. Although she was grateful for the chance to earn some extra money, she could hardly bear the thought of Gavin and Shireen spending the evening together . . . without her. She felt strangely jealous that *her* best friend would be out with *her* boyfriend while she had to work. She wondered if she should ring Gavin and suggest that the cinema visit be put on hold for another evening. Then she decided to call Shireen instead.

'Oh, no,' said Shireen. 'Then let's leave it till you're free, Alison. I've got plenty of things I can do tonight.' Her mind raced. She had *nothing* to do . . . except to finish the already over-long letter to Michael.

'No,' replied Alison, firmly. 'You and Gavin go. He'll be picking you up just after seven.'

'But, I can't!' said Shireen. 'We can't go without you. It isn't fair.'

'What's the point in Gavin spending the evening alone?' she asked. 'He'll only be getting up to all sorts of mischief. I'd rather you were with him, to keep an eye on him.'

'Well, if you're sure?' asked Shireen.

'I'll see you at that coffee bar opposite the cinema about ten o'clock,' concluded Alison. 'Must go. My money's running out.'

She replaced the receiver and wiped the sweat from her top lip. Her hands were trembling. She'd never felt jealous before. Never. She'd never had any *reason* to feel jealous. Not ever. And she couldn't understand why she was feeling this way now. *Why* was she jealous? Shireen wasn't interested in Gavin, that was for sure. And Gavin wasn't interested in Shireen. Was he? *Was* he?

★ ★ ★

Michael placed his linen napkin beside his plate and sat back in his chair feeling satisfied, not only with the splendid meal served by the two rather grumpy maids, but also with his dinner conversation with Antonio and Suzana which had been conducted mainly in Spanish.

'You speak very good Spanish, Michael,' Antonio informed him, with a beaming smile. 'In five weeks' time, you will be fluent.'

118

'*Gracias*,' replied Michael. 'I hope so.'

'And have you any plans for this evening?' asked Suzana.

Michael looked at his watch. It was ten o'clock. As far as he was concerned, the evening was over, although it was still light outside. 'I thought I might watch a bit of television and then go to bed,' he said.

Antonio guffawed. 'You English! As we Spaniards go out to enjoy ourselves, you English go to sleep.'

Suzana agreed. 'You're in Spain now, Michael. You must live as the Spanish do. The evening has only just begun.'

'Besides,' added Antonio, 'it's too hot to sleep.'

Michael smiled. 'You've convinced me. Where can I go?'

'We'll take you to The Torito,' suggested Suzana. 'It's a bar, a short walk away. Typically Spanish.'

'And full of young people,' added Antonio. 'So we will take you there . . . and you can talk to people of your own age.'

'In Spanish, of course,' grinned Suzana.

'In Spanish. Definitely!' smiled Michael.

★ ★ ★

Alison arrived at the coffee bar and stared across at the foyer, waiting for the film to end and for the cinema-goers to emerge into the warm summer's evening. It was dark now, but the air was clear, the sky filled with stars. A glorious summer's night. And here she was, waiting, sipping on yet another Coke, sniffing her fingers and hoping that they didn't smell of hamburgers and french fries and fillet o' fish. As the cinema suddenly began to turn out its crowd, she scanned the figures under the foyer's bright lights, wondering if she'd see Gavin arm in arm with Shireen. She watched cuddling couples hurrying down the steps towards their cars, the bus stops and the taxi-rank. And then she saw the familiar heads; ginger and blonde, in intense conversation, a conversation that she wasn't to be part of. And she sighed with relief when she saw that they weren't arm in arm or hand in hand. They began to cross the road towards the coffee bar and when Shireen saw her best friend perched on a stool in the window, she smiled, waved frantically and raced across towards her.

Gavin immediately wrapped his arm

around Alison's neck and kissed her on the cheek.

'So, how was it?' asked Alison.

Gavin turned up his nose. 'Not very good, was it?' he asked Shireen.

'Bit slushy,' she replied. 'All right, I suppose if you're watching it with someone special . . . ' She giggled. 'Now, if Michael had been with me . . . '

Gavin laughed. 'But she had to put up with me.'

Alison smiled.

'I'll get some coffees,' he said as he headed for the counter.

Shireen sat on the stool beside Alison. 'You must be tired,' she said.

'I am. But at least I'm not working tomorrow.' She sighed. 'Thank goodness it's Sunday. I've got the whole day off . . . and the evening too.'

'Hey, great!' said Shireen. 'We should *do* something.' She stopped. 'Sorry,' she said. 'How stupid. You'll want to spend the day with Gavin.'

She did want to spend the day with Gavin. The whole day. And the evening. Just the two of them. 'No . . . no, of course I don't,' she stammered. 'We can all do something together.'

'We could go to town for the day,' suggested Shireen. 'I was thinking. Perhaps we should go round to Michael's house and meet Pedro. I promised Michael that I'd call on him. We could take him into London to see the sights. What do you think?'

Alison beamed. She felt a sudden calm sweep over her. A foursome. She and Gavin. Shireen and Pedro. It sounded perfect. 'What a good idea,' she said.

★　★　★

The Torito, serving coffee and all kinds of wines and spirits, was full and extremely noisy. Michael had already noted, in his short time in Spain, that they were a very noisy nation. It wasn't so much that the bar's music was being played over-loudly, it was just that the excitable voices of the customers, screeching and shouting across to each other, drowned out any conversation that he and Antonio and Suzana attempted to make. The tiled floor was littered with tiny sugar packets, biscuit wrappings and cigarette ends. The custom, it appeared, was simply to discard all these things by dropping them on to the floor, rather than to find a suitable waste bin.

Suzana shrugged when Michael questioned her about it. 'It's easier to sweep a floor than to empty bins, don't you think?'

Having left Michael and Suzana sipping on ice-cold orange juices, Antonio crossed the room and spoke to a stocky youth, sweltering in a leather jacket, who was playing the pinball machine. The youth smiled, nodded and finished his game. Then he followed Antonio back to join Michael and Suzana at the bar.

He put out his hand and introduced himself in Spanish. Michael was grateful that, after his short practice with his hosts over dinner, he could understand everything that the boy said to him.

'I'm Santi,' he explained. 'One of Pedro's friends. How are you enjoying your visit to Spain?'

'I haven't seen much of it yet,' Michael replied with a smile. 'I'm still settling in.'

'So you haven't been into the centre of Madrid yet?'

'No.'

'Then we'll go tomorrow,' said Santi. 'It's Sunday. A good day for sightseeing.' He called across the bar to another boy in his late teens, who approached, drink in hand.

'Juan, this is Michael,' he said. 'Pedro's exchange partner. What are you doing tomorrow?'

Juan grinned. 'Nothing.'

'So pass the news around, eh? See how many want to go into the centre for the day. We can all meet at the metro about ten.'

'Ten-thirty,' Juan corrected him. 'It's Sunday. Mass first, eh?'

'For *you*,' laughed Santi.

'Si! Mass for me,' grinned Juan as he toyed with the small cross hanging around his neck. 'Mass and then . . . some fun!' He playfully slapped Michael on the back and then strolled back to join his friends, male and female, on the other side of the bar.

When Antonio and Suzana decided to leave, they persuaded Michael to stay on at the bar.

'It's the best way to learn Spanish,' Antonio suggested. He looked at his watch. 'And besides, it's still early. You stay here, Michael. Enjoy yourself.'

Santi continued to engage Michael in conversation for the rest of the evening, trying at times, unfortunately for Michael, to speak in English. He had great difficulties with the language and Michael found it hard to understand him. Finally, Santi relented and continued the conversation in Spanish, which was a relief to both of them.

At one o'clock Michael decided he really ought to be getting back to the house. He was feeling very tired and he wanted to make sure he was refreshed before his visit to the centre of Madrid in the morning.

'But it's early yet,' said Santi. 'The bar doesn't close until five o'clock. Anyway, it's Saturday night.'

'I'm sure I'll eventually get used to your Spanish ways, Santi,' grinned Michael. 'But it's time I was in my bed.'

Santi laughed and shook his hand. 'See you tomorrow,' he said. 'Ten-thirty. After mass.'

As Michael began to leave the bar, he was struck by the beauty of the girl who was just entering. In her late teens she was tall and slim with thick, curly, dark brown hair which cascaded on to her shoulders. On seeing the blond, blue-eyed stranger, she stopped in her tracks and gave him a smile. Flicking back her hair with her fingertips, she stared at him, her dark green eyes twinkling in the lights from the pinball machine.

'Hi!' she said.

'Hi!' he replied.

'Conchita!' a man's voice called from across the bar.

'*Hola!*' Conchita called back. And flashing another quick smile at Michael, she left him at the door and crossed to greet a group of friends.

Michael walked out into the humid, starlit night and, threading his way through the narrow streets, accompanied by the distant sound of a dog baying at the moon . . . and backed by the cicadas gently crooning to each other, he slowly and contentedly made his way home.

10

Michael was woken by the high-pitched buzz of a mosquito, hungrily searching the bedroom for some breakfast. Determined that the breakfast wasn't going to be *him*, he leapt out of bed and headed for the shower, glancing at his watch on the way and noting that it was still only six o'clock. Michael had never seen six o'clock on a Sunday morning at home, but then, in England, most mornings were grey, making another two or three hours under the duvet appear so tempting. Even with the unusually gloriously hot summer they'd been having back home, six o'clock was never quite as sweaty as this.

Having at last managed to dry off, without even needing to use a towel, he put on his blue shorts and white T-shirt before slipping his trainers on to his sockless feet and heading for the kitchen.

He was surprised to find Antonio and Suzana seated at the breakfast table, sipping freshly percolated coffee as they flicked through the Sunday newspapers.

They looked up at him and smiled.

'Up so soon?' asked Suzana as she rose to fetch another cup for her house-guest. 'Or have you only just come in from The Torito?'

Michael laughed. 'I'm English!' he said. 'Remember? I was in bed by one-thirty.'

'You can help yourself to breakfast today,' Antonio informed him. 'The maids don't work on Sundays. They're good Catholic women and they like to attend mass twice today.'

Michael poured some coffee for himself. 'Don't you two go to church?' he asked.

'No,' replied Antonio. 'Pedro used to go, but it wasn't his faith that took him there.'

'Oh?' asked Michael. He was curious.

'It was a girl,' explained Suzana. 'Her family are devout Catholics and she felt that Pedro would be more accepted by her family if he attended the church.'

'So does Pedro still have this girlfriend?' asked Michael.

'No. Unfortunately,' replied Suzana. 'They don't talk any more. And that's a shame, because she was very nice.'

★ ★ ★

Following his hosts' directions, Michael made his way to the old church which stood at the end of the narrow Calle de la Iglesia, its bells tolling and the sun glinting welcomingly off its pale yellow façade. Dozens of people, young and old, were climbing the steep steps to the large portal where they were greeted by the priest, who seemed to know each and every one of them. As Michael passed him, the priest smiled and looked quizzically at him as if to ask, who *is* this stranger?

'*Hola!*' Michael said to him as he entered the church and took his place in one of the back pews. The church was almost full. The sound of the bells mixed unmusically with both the hymn being hammered out on the organ and the cries of the many young babes in arms. Some of the older women had their heads covered in black shawls and each of the congregation genuflected before the altar as they took their seats.

Michael noted the splendour of the church; its golden altar, the paintings and statuettes and the magnificent stained-glass windows, the pictures of which, bathed behind by such glorious sunlight, seemed to be almost alive. His eyes followed the pews as he searched for the lad called Juan whom he'd met in The Torito and who'd said that he had to attend mass this morning.

He saw him seated at the front beside the tall, dark-haired Spanish beauty who had entered the bar as he was leaving ... and he realized immediately that they must be lovers. She sat very close to him, occasionally turning to smile as she touched his arm.

Michael remembered her name. Conchita. Conchita, with the sparkling green eyes, who'd stared at him so strangely. Dressed in black this morning, she looked every inch the story-book Spanish señorita. And as she lifted her black fan to her cheek and flicked it open with such elegance, Michael smiled. This was the Spanish imagery of poetry books; the Spain, which he'd assumed had long since disappeared into the annals of history.

★   ★   ★

At the end of the service, he left the church confused at the ritual he'd just witnessed. At first he was concerned as to why he couldn't understand what the

130

priest was saying. He could recognize only two or three words in every sentence. Surely his Spanish wasn't *that* bad. Hadn't Suzana and Antonio told him that he spoke very good Spanish? He soon realized that the service was being conducted in Latin.

He found Santi standing on the steps, grinning wildly.

'So you are a Catholic too!' said Santi.

Michael shook his hand. 'Good morning,' he said. 'No, I'm not a Catholic, Santi. I'm here out of curiosity.'

Santi was delighted to be able to use one of the colloquial phrases passed on to him by his English teacher at school. 'Curiosity killed the cat!' He guffawed loudly.

'I hope it doesn't kill inquisitive foreigners,' replied Michael with a smile.

'I'm waiting for Conchita and Juan,' explained Santi. He winked at Michael, 'They are both very good Catholics.'

'Yes, I saw them in there,' replied Michael.

'You know Conchita?' Santi was surprised.

'No,' said Michael. 'I saw her very briefly last night.'

'She's beautiful, no?' asked Santi.

'Very,' said Michael.

'I will go to their house with them while Conchita gets changed,' he went on. 'She won't go into the centre in her black.' He laughed. 'She looks like a young window. You can come with us to their home and then we will all go to the metro.'

Michael was shocked. 'So, Juan and Conchita live together?'

Santi smiled. 'Yes. Why not?'

'But if she's a devout Catholic . . . ?' He stopped suddenly, wondering, 'They're not married, surely? They're so young.'

Santi laughed. 'They're brother and sister,' he said. 'They live with their parents.'

Michael suddenly felt relieved. And he wasn't sure why he should feel this way. Why should it bother him? He had no interest in the dusky beauty with the sparkling green eyes. He cared only for Shireen. Nobody could hold a candle to her. And he wished that she were here with him now, on the church steps as the congregation emerged, full of grace. His mind wandered. He could almost feel her presence. Shireen. Shireen and him. Arm in arm. Laughing in the sun and listening to the bells, as they both imbibed a typical Spanish Sunday.

Santi grabbed Michael's arm. 'I thought he may have told you,' he said. 'I thought Pedro may have said something.'

'Told me what?' asked Michael.

'About him and Conchita,' explained Santi. 'They were very much in love. They are *still* very much in love.'

Michael gasped. 'Pedro and Conchita?'

'*Si!* But Conchita says her parents wouldn't approve of him as a future son-in-law. He has no faith, you see. I'm sure that Conchita is wrong. Her parents seem to adore Pedro. But she says they want her to marry a good Catholic boy. And *she* should know.'

'But if they love each other?' Michael couldn't understand why they would split up if they really wanted to be together, no matter what Conchita's parents thought.

'Conchita begged him to go back to the church . . . even if it was just a show! But Pedro is stubborn. Like a mule. He wouldn't do as Conchita asked.'

'But he has every right,' Michael said.

'I agree,' said Santi. 'Anyway, there was a terrible argument. And Conchita told Pedro that the relationship was over.'

'Oh. That's sad,' said Michael. 'And so stupid if you ask me.'

Santi shrugged and sighed heavily. 'Now both Conchita and Pedro are broken-hearted and I believe it's all for nothing. I'm sure Conchita's parents wouldn't disapprove of Pedro. But obviously, that's what Conchita believes.'

Their conversation came to an abrupt end when Juan and Conchita emerged from the church. Conchita was introduced to Michael and as she greeted him with a kiss on the cheek, he smelt her sweet perfume and immediately felt a cold sweat break out on his forehead. This was followed by a deep sense of guilt. He quickly closed his eyes and pictured Shireen, wrapped in his arms beside the crackling bonfire in the dark, Kent countryside.

★ ★ ★

The boys sat in the front garden of Conchita and Juan's old farmhouse where, shaded by the crumbling olive tree, which had long ceased to bear fruit, they waited. Michael hoped to catch sight of the parents, the villains in the romantic tale of

134

Conchita and Pedro . . . the modern-day story of the Montagues and Capulets.

'Are your parents still at mass?' Michael eventually asked Juan.

'They are in Andalucia, visiting relatives,' explained Juan. 'They are Sevillanos.'

Michael looked blank.

Santi explained. 'Conchita and Juan's parents were born in Seville. They came north to find work many years ago. And they've remained here for thirty years.'

Juan laughed. 'Santi is sick of hearing my parents talk of the wonderful times in Seville. They are always promising to return there someday.'

'Would you and Conchita ever move south?' asked Michael.

'Never,' replied Juan. 'Andalucia is truly beautiful. But there is very little work there.'

'And Juan and I are Madrileños,' said a soft voice from behind them. 'We were born in Madrid. This is our home.'

Michael looked up to see Conchita, now dressed in scarlet; matching dress and shoes, her hair tumbling beautifully about her shoulders. In her hand she carried a green fan, while a small white bag hung over one arm.

'*Vámanos!*' she said. 'Let's go!'

* ★ ★ ★

No one else had arrived at the metro by ten-thirty, which didn't surprise Santi. They waited until eleven, as none of their friends, like most Spaniards, were good timekeepers.

'The English are always early,' said Juan. 'The Germans are always on time. And the Spanish never look at their watches.'

At eleven-thirty, they decided to make the journey into the centre of Madrid alone. Just the four of them: Michael, Santi, Juan . . . and the stunningly beautiful Conchita.

As they approached The Rastro market, all heads turned to stare at the girl in the red dress . . . and the blond-haired, blue-eyed foreigner walking beside her.

The Rastro was packed; the long street was lined with stalls and heaving with wall-to-wall people. It was impossible to move more than a few metres without being held up by the throng. Michael continually removed his shades, wiping the sweat from his stinging eyes and cursing that he hadn't brought his cap to prevent the fierce rays from blistering his scalp. They passed stalls selling all sorts of goods: rugs, furniture, clothes, food, plants . . . and all types of exotic looking birds in cramped wooden cages.

Conchita stopped at a jewellery stall and bartered in rapid Spanish with the stallholder as she held up a pair of crystal earrings. Finally, she threw them down in disgust, obviously believing that the price being asked was far too high. Then, as they began to move off, Michael noticed the tiny gold cross lying on a purple pin-cushion. Realizing that his Spanish wasn't good enough to barter, he asked Conchita to do it for him and, satisfied with the price, he paid the stallholder and pocketed the cross.

Conchita looked at him, enquiringly.

★ ★ ★

Michael's mother was pleased when Shireen arrived to ask if Pedro would like to accompany her and her two friends to London for the day. She'd feared that she'd have to keep the teenage Spaniard occupied when, having been at work all week, she felt that she would have preferred to sit in the garden, reading the Sunday newspapers.

'I'm sure he'll be delighted,' she said. 'I'll just go and tell him you're here.'

Shireen strolled down the garden path towards the gate, where Alison and Gavin waited, hand in hand.

'I hope he's all right,' said Alison. 'I mean, can he speak English? We're going to have a terrible day if we can't communicate with him, aren't we?'

'Of course he can speak English,' replied Shireen. 'He's been learning it at school. He's over here to improve it, that's all.'

The window at the top of the house opened and a voice called out. 'Hello. I'm Pedro. *Momento, por favor!*'

Shireen looked up, shielding her eyes from the bright sunlight, trying to get a good look at the boy whose photo she'd already seen. He disappeared from view and closed the window.

Alison gasped, looked at Shireen and giggled. 'Did you see him?' she asked.

'No. Not really,' replied Shireen.

'*I* did,' said Gavin, huffily.

'What's the matter, Gavin?' asked Shireen.

'Nothing,' he replied, flatly.

Alison shrieked with laughter. 'I think Gavin was a bit jealous,' she said. She mock-whispered to Shireen, 'Our young Pedro looks a bit tasty.'

'Don't be ridiculous!' snapped Gavin. 'I'm not in the slightest bit jealous.'

'And it wouldn't matter to me how 'tasty' Pedro is,' smiled Shireen. 'We're just being nice to him for Michael's sake.' She wagged a finger at Alison, as a joke warning, 'So just you remember that, Alison.'

'*Moi?*' giggled Alison. '*I'm* not interested in him. Why should I be?' She cuddled up to Gavin. 'Not when I've got my tall redhead to hold on to. It's *you* I'm worried about, Shireen. After all, it's *you* who's going to be alone for five weeks.'

'*Hola!*' yelled Pedro as he hurried down the path towards them, dressed in red shorts and baggy white T-shirt.

Shireen stared, open-mouthed at the handsome face, the dark brown eyes below the short, jet-black hair, the dazzling white smile . . . and the strong, tanned legs.

'Hi!' she gulped. 'So you're Pedro!'

11

On the train to Charing Cross, the four chatted constantly, and when they'd arrived, it felt, strangely, as though Pedro had always been part of their lives. He was extremely easy to talk to and had a sense of humour which appealed to them all, particularly to Gavin. Shireen was keen to know about Pedro's home life, knowing that this would enable her to picture Michael more easily, in his new environment.

'Hey! I almost forgot,' said Pedro as he rummaged in the shoulder-bag he was carrying. 'Michael sent this to you.' He handed the sealed envelope to Shireen, whose heart suddenly began to pound, rapidly.

'A love letter!' shrieked Alison. 'What's it say?'

Gavin took Alison's hand and squeezed it affectionately. 'I think Shireen may want to keep that to herself, don't you?'

'I'll look at it later,' said Shireen, who was bursting to open it. She tucked it into the back pocket of her jeans, hoping that there would be a quiet moment in the day when she would be able to read it in private.

Heading along The Strand, they reached Covent Garden, which was bustling with tourists, some Americans but mainly Europeans . . . and here they decided to take coffee at one of the pavement cafés.

Pedro, struck by Shireen's beauty, made a concerted effort to take in all three of his companions as he talked to them, aware that, at first, Shireen had received too much attention from him. He'd even found himself, at one stage, on the edge of flirting with her, although he was sure that she hadn't realized what he was doing. He stopped immediately. He didn't want to offend her . . . nor her friends.

Besides, from the way that Shireen had talked about Michael on their journey to town, it was obvious that she was very much in love with him. Any advances from Pedro, no matter how slight, would be spurned. That was for sure.

He remembered that this was how he used to behave before he met Conchita: flirting with any pretty girl he came across. She'd changed all that. As soon as their relationship had begun, he hadn't looked at anyone else. What was the point? Conchita was everything he wanted. She was beautiful, strong-willed and fun to be with. And he'd felt sure that they'd always be together. To dump him, unceremoniously, as she did, had come as a terrible shock.

He still couldn't believe it had happened. When she'd said it was all over, it was like a dagger to his heart. And when the offer of the exchange visit to London was offered, he'd leapt at the chance, hoping that by distancing himself from her and all their mutual friends, it might give him the time he needed for the wounds to heal. Now he was a free agent. He could, if he wished, return to his old ways. And if only Shireen wasn't so in love with Michael, then . . .

As the waiter placed the ordered cups of coffee on to their table, Shireen asked him where the toilets were.

'I won't be a minute,' she said to the others. Then, as soon as she was in private, she opened Michael's letter and began to read:

★ ★ ★

Dear Shireen,

I'm missing you already. I just thought I'd let you know that I'm not living in a shack. The house is beautiful and is on the outskirts of Madrid. I have my own room with an en suite shower and, would you believe it, I have maids to cook and clean up after me. It's incredible the way some people live, isn't it? I think I'm going to be happy here. Fairly happy. My happiness could only be complete if you were here with me. I just keep thinking of all the things we could do together, if only you could have come to Spain too. It just seems ridiculous for you to spend your summer there, alone in London, especially as your parents will be going away to France. And here, there are so many bedrooms. What do you think? Is there any chance that you could come over? Pedro's parents, Antonio and Suzana, are so nice. I'm sure they'd be happy about having another house-guest. Anyway, please think about it. Seriously. It would be great if you were with me. Pedro seems very nice, I must say. By the time you read this, you will, of course, have met him. Handsome, isn't he? I hope you don't fall for him. I'm sure he'll go mad when he sees you. But then, who wouldn't? I miss you and love you and can't wait till we're back together again.

All my love, for ever.
Michael.

Shireen sighed, put the letter back into its envelope and slipped it into her pocket. Her mind was racing. Was there a chance of going to Spain? She had some savings in her post office account. So that was no problem. But she was pretty sure her parents wouldn't approve. They liked Michael, but there was no way they'd let her go to Spain to join him. Still, there was no harm in asking. She'd do it tonight.

'Your coffee's cold,' said Gavin as Shireen returned, looking slightly flushed.

'I expect you've been reading Lover Boy's letter, haven't you?' asked Alison, twinkling. 'So, what's it say?'

'Alison!' Gavin reprimanded her.

Shireen smiled and sipped on the cold coffee, saying nothing.

★ ★ ★

Sunday in Madrid's beautiful Retiro Park was the most popular day for the strolling Madrileños. Juan grabbed a table at the café facing the great lake and all four sat under the shade of a parasol, ordering a lunch of cold drinks and *tapas*.

Michael took out the tiny gold cross from his pocket and placed it on the table. Then, releasing the catch from Shireen's gold chain around his neck, he removed it and carefully slipped the cross on to it.

Conchita watched him, wide-eyed. 'Are you a Catholic?' she asked.

Michael was surprised at her question. 'No. Why?'

'Oh.' She sounded disappointed. 'I saw you at Mass. And I thought that the gold cross . . . '

Michael began to put the chain around his neck. 'No. This is for someone special,' he explained. 'And I only went to Mass because I was curious.'

'But you *believe*,' she said. 'You have faith. You must believe, or you wouldn't wear a cross.'

'I'm not sure what I believe,' replied Michael almost dismissively. 'I'm wearing this chain simply because it was given to me by someone I love very much.'

The waiter arrived with a tray of drinks and half a dozen small white dishes which he placed on the table.

'What are these?' Michael asked as he stared, with some trepidation, into the dishes.

'A mixture of all sorts,' grinned Santi, aware that most Englishmen would rather tuck into burgers and fries than anchovies or garlic-soaked olives.

Michael picked up the tiny fork and dug into the anchovy dish, dropping a few of them into his mouth and grimacing at the taste.

'They're so salty,' he said as he quickly washed them down with a mouthful of Coke.

Conchita laughed and took a forkful of peas and chopped ham. 'This will be better for your delicate English tongue,' she said as she leaned forwards and placed the fork at Michael's lips. He took them into his mouth . . . and chewed.

'Better?' she asked.

'Much,' he grinned.

There was the sound of a tambourine and looking up they saw a young girl, hand in hand with a clownish figure dressed in white.

'It's a pierrot,' Conchita shrieked excitedly.

The young girl took a step back as the clown began, in silence, to perform his magic tricks. He produced silk scarves and cards and eventually a small white dove from his sleeve, to the approval of the crowd now gathering around the café. Then reaching inside his white jacket, the pierrot placed his hand on his heart and peeled off a small red balloon which he began to inflate by the use of a tiny pump. The balloon slowly expanded until it resembled a large red love-heart.

'Aaah!' said the crowd as one, before laughing and then applauding loudly.

The pierrot tied a piece of string on to the heart-shaped balloon and then handed it to the smiling Conchita before moving off to find another audience on the other side of the park. His young female companion lingered for a while, holding out her tambourine and gratefully receiving the few pesetas which some of the audience placed there.

Conchita looked wistfully at the balloon.

'Why do I think you're thinking of Pedro?' asked Juan.

Conchita immediately let go of the balloon, and the four of them watched it as it sailed into the air and across the lake. 'Perhaps your heart will fly all the way to London,' Juan said softly.

'Perhaps,' Conchita replied.

★   ★   ★

From Covent Garden, Pedro was led to Trafalgar Square by his English guides, on towards Buckingham Palace and then back to Green Park where they strolled along the water's edge, watching the ducks and moorhens frolicking in the sun. As they crossed the tiny bridge, Alison spied a discarded lolly-stick and screeching with delight, she picked it up and dropped it over the side, watching the water below carry it under the bridge and out of view. She and Gavin then peered over the other side of the bridge and waited, like two young children, for their stick to reappear on top of the fast-flowing water.

'There it is!' screamed Alison.

Shireen looked at Pedro and tutted. 'They're like two kids.'

Pedro questioned her, 'Kids? Baby goats?'

Shireen laughed. 'Yes. Baby goats.'

As Alison and Gavin busied themselves looking for more debris to throw over the bridge, Shireen took the opportunity to inform Pedro of Michael's suggestion.

'I think it's a very good idea,' replied Pedro. He gazed into her eyes, seeing only Conchita's eyes looking back at him. Secretly he hoped that she wouldn't go to Spain. It was exciting being in the company of someone as beautiful as Shireen. Exciting, but dangerous. 'I'm absolutely sure that my parents wouldn't mind,' he added. 'We have plenty of room and they're both very free-thinking people. I think they would welcome you with open arms.'

Shireen began to tremble with excitement. Was it possible? Could she spend the summer with Michael in Madrid?

'Hey!' yelped Gavin suddenly. 'Who wants an ice-cream?'

Alison had also noted the ice-cream stall set up outside the park gates. 'Me, please!' she said.

'I'll come with you, Gavin,' said Pedro.

'The two girls can stay here and throw sticks into the water like . . . baby goats.'

As they watched Gavin and Pedro amble towards the gates, Alison whispered, as though it were some great secret. 'He really is dishy, isn't he?'

Shireen laughed. 'I assume you mean your Gavin?'

'Oh, he's lovely, is Gavin,' replied Alison. 'I wouldn't swap him for the world. But no, I wasn't talking about Gavin, Shireen.'

'Yes, he's very handsome,' agreed Shireen. 'When Michael showed me the photo I knew that he was quite good-looking, but . . . '

'And he's certainly taken a fancy to you,' chortled Alison.

'Don't be ridiculous,' laughed Shireen. 'What makes you say that?'

'He doesn't take his eyes off you,' said Alison. 'Every time I look at him, he's staring at you.'

'Nonsense!' she said. 'You're making it up.'

'You'll see,' grinned Alison. 'I bet he makes a move on you. Just give him a few days.'

Shireen glared at Alison. 'I don't want him to make a move on me, as you so delicately put it, Alison. I'm not in the slightest bit interested in him. Anyway, I may not be here for much longer.'

Alison was shocked. 'What do you mean?'

'That letter. From Michael.'

'Yes?'

'He's asked me to go out to join him in Spain.'

'No!' Alison gasped. 'And?'

'I'd love to, but I'll have to ask my mum and dad.'

Alison shook her head, sadly. 'They'll never let you. You know how protective your parents are. They won't let you go off abroad on your own.'

'Well, I'm going to try,' said Shireen. She looked up at Alison, with tears in her eyes. 'I don't think I can stand five weeks without him. I'm going to ask my mum and dad tonight.'

'Well, I'll keep my fingers crossed for you,' said Alison. 'But don't raise your hopes.'

★ ★ ★

151

Shireen waited until her father had left for his nightly visit to the pub, before broaching the subject.

'I had a letter from Michael today,' she said to her mother. Her mouth was dry. She sipped on her coffee and continued. 'His exchange partner, Pedro, had brought it over for me.'

Shireen's mother pointed the remote control at the TV screen and changed channels, only half-listening to her daughter. 'That was nice of him,' she said.

'Anyway, he's living in this really big place . . .'

'Don't want this, do we?' Mum asked, referring to the TV programme.

'Erm . . . I don't mind,' replied Shireen.

Mum pressed the control again.

'So, I wanted to tell you something, while Dad was out. Well, *ask* you something, really.'

Mum suddenly began to pay attention. She feared what she was going to hear. She turned off the TV's sound and put down the remote control. 'What?'

'It's just that . . .'

'There's nothing wrong, is there?' Mum was concerned.

'No. There's nothing wrong.'

'But this is to do with you and Michael?'

'Yes.'

Shireen's mother's eyes widened. She began to pale slightly. 'You're not . . . ?'

Shireen was annoyed. 'No! I'm not. Don't be ridiculous. I'm not stupid, Mum!'

Mum guiltily looked back at the silent screen. 'Sorry. I just thought for a minute . . . '

'Michael has asked if I'll go to Spain,' Shireen blurted out. 'There's plenty of room in the house and . . . '

'No!' her mother replied, firmly, 'Definitely not.'

'But why?' It was the answer that she'd expected, but she was hoping to talk her mother round.

'You can't come to France with us,' snapped her mother, 'but you can go off to Spain to spend time with a boy you've known for five minutes!'

'Mum!' pleaded Shireen. 'Think about it. Please. It'll be a great experience for me . . . and once I start college I may not get another chance like this.'

'No!' said her mother. 'And it's no good

trying to soft-soap me while your father's out, because we'd both agree about this one. You're not going. And I don't want to hear any more about it.'

Shireen silently left the room.

12

During the ten days that he'd been in Madrid, Michael had spent most of his time in the company of Conchita, although Juan was always nearby, acting as a chaperone to his younger sister. Both were on holiday from college, free to show Michael the areas around Madrid which he'd never have seen without them. Santi joined them most evenings, but during the day he had to work — a school holiday job in the local bakery, which he continuously complained about.

Michael had seen and learnt the history of Toledo, Escorial and The Valley Of The Fallen and with help from his new friends, he'd found that his Spanish had improved tremendously. Even Antonio and Suzana had dropped their 'Spanglish' and were now only speaking to him in Spanish. They hoped that Pedro, who seemed to be enjoying his stay in London, was working as hard as Michael at improving his language skills.

Shireen's letter had sorely disappointed Michael.

He'd been so excited about everything he'd seen and done and although he'd try to share his excitement in the letters he regularly sent to her, he longed for her to be by his side, tasting the delights of Spain with him. He thought about her constantly, even though there were times, when in deep conversation with Conchita, he'd felt he wanted to reach out and take the beautiful Spanish girl in his arms. These desires were immediately followed by feelings of profound guilt. He loved Shireen so much and he knew he could never do anything to hurt her. But Conchita's dark green eyes, staring into his, as she chatted and smiled and playfully stroked his arm, were almost . . . hypnotic.

★ ★ ★

On his one day off Santi had borrowed his father's car and had offered to take his three friends on an adventure drive. They met at El Torito in time for morning coffee and set off around eleven o'clock, leaving Madrid and driving through the tunnel towards Segovia. As Juan had decided to ride in the front passenger seat, Michael sat in the back beside Conchita, who today was dressed in khaki shorts and a pale green T-shirt. She wore no make-up and her pale olive face shone as the morning heat grew in intensity. Michael felt the sweat running down the back of his legs and was grateful that he'd decided to wear his shorts rather than his jeans.

As they approached the huge Roman aqueduct at the entrance into the city, Michael felt Conchita's leg brushing against his. At first he was sure that it was Santi's erratic stop-start driving which had simply forced Conchita to change position in the bumpy back seat. He waited for her to move her leg. She didn't. He was sure that she was pressing it closer to his. He began to sweat even more, wondering if he should move away from her, fearful that Juan, gazing through the windscreen at the magnificent aqueduct, would become aware of his laboured breathing. He tentatively reached across and placed his hand on top of Conchita's, waiting for her to brush it aside with a giggle.

There was a deathly silence for minutes, both of them now peering out of their respective backseat windows, admiring the scenery. Finally, he felt her gently squeeze his hand. He responded by doing the same, as he turned to look at her. She gave no reaction. He wondered what was going on in her mind. And he feared that behind her dark shades, those hypnotic green eyes were laughing at him.

'Beautiful, isn't she?' said Juan, quite suddenly.

Michael immediately withdrew his hand.

'The aqueduct,' added Juan. 'Beautiful, isn't she? A stunning piece of architecture.'

'She's *extremely* beautiful,' replied Michael. He looked at Conchita, sure that she'd respond with a smile. She didn't move. Staring straight ahead she sighed deeply . . . and Michael watched as a tear ran from under her shades and down her cheek.

★ ★ ★

Alison was extremely disappointed that on the day they'd all chosen to travel to the Sussex coast, the flu-bug had caused a staff shortage at McDonald's and the manager had asked her to work. She rang

Gavin's home and suggested they all went without her.

'I don't want to go without you,' said Gavin, plaintively. 'Can't your refuse? Can't you say that you've got the flu too?'

'I can't, Gavin,' she replied. 'They're in such a state here.'

'But *I've* got to go, Alison; you do realize that, don't you? They'll be so disappointed if I cancel now.'

'I know,' she said. 'Of course you've got to go with them. But as you're walking along Brighton beach, just you think about me saying, 'Enjoy your meal,' for the thousandth time.'

Gavin laughed. 'I'll miss you,' he said.

'Yes. Just make sure that you do,' she replied with a chuckle. 'I'll see you tomorrow.'

★ ★ ★

Passing through the narrow, higgledy-piggledy streets of Segovia, they finally took their seats at a pavement café and gazed up at the distant Alcazar, with its conical towers making it appear like some sort of Disneyland castle.

'I'm half expecting Mickey Mouse to

come skipping along the road and grab my hand,' said Michael.

'It's a bit older than Disneyland, Michael,' grinned Santi. 'And its stories aren't so cosy. It's perched on the side of a deep precipice and in the fourteenth century a nanny accidently dropped a baby she was looking after, over the edge.'

'How clumsy of her,' grinned Michael.

His Spanish companions didn't laugh.

'She was so distressed', continued Santi, 'that she threw herself over the edge too. No, it certainly isn't Disneyland,' he added.

Michael couldn't take his eyes from the structure. It was the picture he'd seen in every childhood story-book. The castle where the Prince finally took Snow White to live happily ever after. The home of Cinderella's Prince Charming. The castle where Sleeping Beauty lay asleep for a hundred years until her prince woke her with a kiss.

'It's an amazing building,' said Juan, as he grabbed the camera from his bag. 'I'm going to take some photos. Coming?'

'Later,' replied Conchita. 'I want to finish my coffee.'

Santi followed Juan. 'We'll meet you at

the top of the hill when you're ready,' he called back.

Michael nodded at them with a smile, but didn't attempt to move. He had to be alone with Conchita for a few minutes. He had to find out what had been going through her mind when she'd gently squeezed his hand.

Left alone with him, she was obviously embarrassed.

He tried to make light of the situation, joking, 'You'd look good in that fairy-tale castle. The Sleeping Beauty's got nothing on you.'

She didn't reply.

'Being woken up by some handsome prince . . . '

She sighed.

'What's wrong, Conchita?' he asked her, softly.

She refused to look at him, staring ahead at the passers-by. 'Nothing's wrong.'

'Please,' he said. 'Talk to me. Tell me why you did that. Tell me what's making you so unhappy.'

She slowly removed her sunglasses and turned to face him. Her eyes were cloudy. 'Oh, Michael,' she tried to explain, speaking in English. 'I'm very sorry. I think you may have misunderstood me. I should never have held your hand like that. I don't want you to think . . . ' She stopped and looked away again.

'Think what?' he replied, also in English. 'That you were coming on to me?'

She smiled. 'Coming on to me? What does that mean?'

He smiled too. 'I don't know how to say it in Spanish. So perhaps it's better if I don't try to translate it, eh?'

'I miss Pedro so much,' she said, suddenly. 'I love him, Michael. And I'm so very, very lonely without him.'

Michael was stunned into silence.

'Every day I miss him. And I wish I could go back a few months . . . when everything was all right.'

'But a few months back or a few years forward, the problem will still be there, Conchita,' he said. 'Your parents can't force him into a religion he doesn't believe in.'

'I know,' she said. 'The problem will always remain, Michael.'

He shook his head in despair. 'I really don't understand,' he said.

She stood, her sunglasses dangling

delicately from one hand and began to walk away from him. 'No. I don't suppose you do,' she replied.

He followed her. 'Conchita!'

She stopped. 'We'd better go and join the others,' she said.

He firmly gripped both her arms in his hands and stared into her eyes. 'Conchita,' he said softly.

'Michael,' she replied, 'don't. Please.'

He kissed her . . . and he felt no response. He stepped back and looked at her, deeply ashamed. 'Sorry,' he said. 'I'm very sorry.'

She lowered her voice to a whisper. 'You love Shireen. And in spite of everything, I still love Pedro. I always will.'

'Yes, I know,' he said. 'I'm sorry.'

'So, let's forget this happened, eh?' she suggested. 'And now, we really must go and find Santi and Juan.'

★ ★ ★

Gavin wandered along the promenade behind Shireen and Pedro, wishing that Alison had been able to accompany them. At times he stopped to watch the children splashing about in the sea or filling up

163

their buckets with pebbles. And whenever he stopped, he was aware that Pedro and Shireen simply strolled on without him. For most of the time they were oblivious to his presence. And this began to worry him. He was suddenly aware that the two of them appeared to be getting very . . . close. He hoped they weren't becoming *too* close. He began to panic. Surely Shireen hadn't fallen for Pedro? No. She couldn't! That would break Michael's heart.

When they left the promenade and sat on the shingled beach, gazing out at the clear horizon, Gavin sat beside them, saying nothing. He wasn't sure if he should, when he had the chance, let Shireen know of his fears. But then he decided that he'd leave that to Alison. After all, she was Shireen's best friend, and if something had to be said, it would be better coming from her.

He looked at his watch, wondering if it was time they all went and found somewhere to have lunch. Then he remembered. The car. He had to return to the parking meter to put in some more money. He cursed. This day out was costing him a fortune. And while he wouldn't have bothered about the expense if he and Alison were enjoying a day at the coast together, today he felt as though he were being used. He'd been nothing more than a chauffeur. They didn't even seem to want his company now that they'd arrived at their destination.

'I'll be back in a while,' he said. 'I've just got to go and feed the meter.'

'Hang on,' replied Shireen as she searched in her bag for her purse. 'I'll give you some money. I don't see why you should pay for everything, Gavin.'

'And I will pay for the petrol,' added Pedro, 'and buy us all some lunch.'

'Thanks,' said Gavin as he took Shireen's money with a smile and left, feeling guilty. 'I won't be long.'

As he hurried off, Pedro stared after him. 'He's a nice guy,' he said. 'I don't think *I'd* have come all the way to Brighton, if my girlfriend couldn't come with me.'

'Aah, but you don't have a girlfriend,' said Shireen, dismissively.

Pedro fell strangely silent.

Shireen stared at him. 'What's up?' she asked. Then it hit her. She suddenly realized. For the first time in the ten days she'd known him, she was aware that he had someone back home. Someone he cared for. 'You *do*, don't you?' she said. 'You do have a girlfriend?'

'No,' he replied. 'I don't. There is someone who I love very much, but . . . '

Shireen sounded sympathetic. 'But she doesn't love you.' It was a statement, not a question.

'She *does* love me,' argued Pedro. 'We both love each other.'

'But why haven't you told me?' asked Shireen. She immediately felt stupid at asking such a ridiculous question. Why *should* he have told her? It had nothing to do with her.

'Because it has ended,' he said. 'We love each other, but we cannot be together.'

'But why?' asked Shireen.

'It is too difficult,' he said. He looked at her, sadly. 'I don't want to talk about it today. Today it is too nice a day to talk about it. We should enjoy the sunshine and the beach . . . and each other's company. Someday I will tell you.'

'But she *is* Spanish?' asked Shireen.

He sighed. 'Yes. Her name is Conchita and she is very, very beautiful. She lives in Madrid, very near to my house.'

'Really?' Shireen was surprised. 'So Michael's probably met her?'

'Michael *would* have met her, yes,' replied Pedro. 'Without doubt. Conchita and I have many mutual friends. And I'm sure Michael will have met some of them. And therefore he will have met Conchita.'

'And he'll know that you and Conchita were lovers?'

'Yes. I'm sure he'll know,' said Pedro. 'It's not a secret.'

Shireen gazed into space. Her mind was racing. This was all very strange. If Michael had met Pedro's girlfriend, why hadn't he mentioned it in his letters? Unless . . . ?

13

The sun was just beginning to set as Santi drove his companions back towards Madrid. Michael stared in awe through the back window at the blood-red sky and for a brief moment he blocked out the hurt he'd felt when Conchita had insisted on sitting up front with the driver. He'd hoped that they'd both be able to forget the snatched kiss; that they could still be friends. But now he wondered if she'd decided to turn her back on him . . . literally; that they would no longer be spending any time together.

He shivered. Then recovered. Perhaps it was for the best. He still loved Shireen . . . so, so deeply . . . and although this Spanish beauty had, for a while, captivated him, he now knew for certain where his heart lay. He wished that Shireen were with him, gazing out at the sunset, watching the swallows darting to and fro and the large, red kites circling overhead searching for supper. He wanted to share with her this feeling of intoxication, brought about by the wondrous sights and sounds and smells of a great foreign land.

Juan gently dug him with his elbow. 'It's beautiful, eh?'

'Beautiful,' agreed Michael.

'But you've seen nothing yet,' added Juan. 'You haven't seen the *real* Spain.'

Santi looked through his rear-view mirror and sneered jokingly at Juan '*Qué va!*' he said. 'What nonsense! This is *all* the real Spain.'

Juan laughed. 'Santi gets angry when I talk of the *real* Spain, Michael,' he explained. 'He knows I'm talking about Southern Spain; Andalucia.'

'And as I come from Barcelona in the north,' continued Santi, 'I find this a great insult.'

Conchita turned her head to look at Michael, smiling at him for the first time since they'd left Segovia. 'Juan is right,' she said. 'You must see Andalucia while you're here.'

'You must visit Seville,' Juan went on. 'I would never leave Madrid, for sure. That is my home and I love it there. But to visit Seville, the homeland of my parents and my grandparents, is a must for any visitor to Spain.'

Santi tutted. 'Flamenco and gypsies and bullrings.'

'We could take him there, Juan,' Conchita suggested enthusiastically. She addressed Michael. 'We could stay with our grandparents for a few days. Would you like that, Michael? You could meet our parents at the same time.'

'I'd love it,' Michael replied. 'But if your parents are already staying there, will there be enough room? Won't your grandparents mind?'

'There's plenty of room,' said Conchita. 'And my grandparents will be very happy to meet you.' She turned to Santi and teasingly placed her hand on his knee. 'I'm sure Santi could borrow his father's car for a few days.'

Santi shook his head. 'I'm sure he *can't*,' he grinned.

'Then we'll take a bus,' smiled Conchita. '*No hay problema*.'

⋆　⋆　⋆

On their return from Brighton, Gavin, although feeling very tired, offered to drive Shireen and Pedro to their respective homes.

170

'I'm sure you want to go straight off to see Alison,' said Pedro. 'You can drop us both at Shireen's house. I can walk from there.'

'No, it's no problem,' Gavin said quickly while trying to stifle a yawn. 'I'll take you home, Pedro.'

'Don't be silly, Gavin,' said Shireen. 'You've done enough driving for one day. I'm sure Pedro won't mind walking home from my place.'

Gavin began to worry about leaving them alone together. He could think only of the promise he'd made to Michael . . . to look after Shireen. And he wasn't fulfilling that promise!

'I insist,' said Pedro. 'I shall enjoy the walk, Gavin.'

Reluctantly leaving them at Shireen's path, Gavin turned the car around and headed for Alison's house. He'd decided not to tell Alison how concerned he was about Shireen and Pedro. Not tonight. Alison would probably suggest that they went back to Shireen's house on some pretext, just to make sure that Pedro had gone straight home. Gavin sighed. He wanted to protect Michael's interests, but not if it meant interfering with his own relationship with Alison. He'd spent all day with Shireen and Pedro. He'd done all he could. And now it was *his* time. He wanted to be alone with Alison, to hold her in his arms, to ask about her day, to tell her once again that he loved her. He'd certainly tell Alison his fears. But it would have to wait until tomorrow. He didn't want to think about Shireen and Pedro for the next hour or so. He didn't even want to think about Michael.

★   ★   ★

'Would you like to come in for some coffee?' Shireen asked him.

Pedro looked at his watch. 'No. I think I'd better get home. Can I see you tomorrow?' he asked.

'Of course,' she replied. 'I don't know what plans Alison and Gavin have, but I'm sure we can sort out something exciting to do.'

'It's been a very enjoyable day,' he said. 'I really like your company, Shireen. And Gavin's too,' he added quickly, sounding a little embarrassed.

'And *I* like *your* company, Pedro,' Shireen said with a smile. Her heart skipped a beat. She stared into his dark eyes . . . and immediately began to panic. Oh Michael, why aren't you with me, she thought. I don't like what's going on here.

Pedro stepped forward and put his arms around her. 'Are you all right?' he asked. 'You seem a little sad.'

She closed her eyes and pictured Michael wrapping his arms around her, pulling her closer towards him. She could feel his broad chest pressing against hers. She could see his handsome, lightly tanned face below the mop of blond hair . . . and the bright, blue eyes, clouding slightly as he leaned forward to kiss her. She saw him smile and she heard his voice whisper, 'I love you, Shireen.'

'I'm fine, Pedro,' she croaked. 'Honestly, I'm fine.'

'Well, goodnight,' he said softly. He kissed her lightly on the cheek. Then he turned and walked away.

★ ★ ★

Shireen sat at the kitchen table, writing her daily letter to Michael. She could hear her parents crashing around upstairs, packing their cases for their holiday in

France. She wished now that she'd planned to go with them, despite her reservations about camping. At least it would have meant saying goodbye to Pedro . . . before things got out of control! What was the point now, she wondered, in hanging around here without Michael by her side? When she'd originally refused the offer, she'd thought that she and Alison would be having a great time together. But that was before they'd both fallen in love.

Dear Michael,

I've just got back from Brighton and I've had a great day, although naturally it would've been so much better if you'd been there. I really miss you. More than you can imagine. My parents are off to France tomorrow and in a way I wish I was going with them now. Knowing you'd be just down the road in Spain would've made the campsite a little more bearable. Still, it's too late now. Alison and Gavin are a great comfort to me, although Alison spends too much time working, leaving poor Gavin with time on his hands.

Pedro seemed to enjoy Brighton, although I think he found it strange sitting on pebbles rather than those sandy beaches they have in Spain. He's really nice, Michael. I like him a lot. I don't want you to get the wrong idea, but I'm very pleased that you and I are going out together, because if not, I might have got to really like him . . . if you know what I mean. And that would've been a disaster, because of course, he'd have to go back to Spain eventually and that would've been very upsetting . . .

Oh, dear . . . I've just read this letter back and it looks as though I've fallen for Pedro, which I haven't. I was in two minds whether or not to tear it up and start again, but then I thought that that would be dishonest in a way. I'm only telling you my feelings because if we have a future together, we have to be honest with each other and say exactly how we feel. I do find him rather attractive, I must say. You knew I would. But of course, if you were here, I wouldn't have even given him a second glance. Oh, I do love you, Michael. And I wish the days would speed by so that we're back together again. Pedro was *telling me all about his ex-girlfriend called Conchita. He said that you would've met her out there. I'm just surprised that you haven't mentioned her in your letters. I hope it's not because you've fallen for her (ha ha . . . as if you would). Anyway, I'll close now and get this into the post first thing in the morning.*

All my love.
Shireen.

She placed the letter in an envelope, stuck on a stamp and, on the way up to bed, she left it on the hall table beside several other letters waiting to be posted. Her father passed her on the staircase.

'Finished packing?' she asked.

He sighed. 'Nearly. Mum said she'd do the rest. I'm gasping for a pint.'

'You're not going to the pub at this time of night, are you?' she asked, surprised.

He looked at his watch. 'It's only ten o'clock,' he grinned. 'Plenty of time before last orders.'

She passed her parents' bedroom and eyed her mother trying to squeeze a huge bath towel into an already bulging suitcase.

'Night, Mum,' she said and she went into her room and sat on the edge of her bed, thinking. She hoped Michael wouldn't be upset when he read her latest love letter. Perhaps it'd been a bit stupid to be quite so honest. If Michael felt that she was two-timing him ... he'd be distraught. It might ruin the fun he was having in Spain. He might even feel that if *she* had her eye on someone else, then he would do the same. She suddenly felt her breathing becoming shallow. She took a huge gasp of air, trying to control it. Her hands began to tremble. Why hadn't he mentioned Conchita? Surely he wasn't ... ? No. Not Michael.

She lay back on her bed and thought about the wonderful days they'd spent together, particularly the day at Bluebell Wood; sitting beside the fire they'd built as they waited for Gavin's dad to arrive. She closed her eyes and slept.

★   ★   ★

She woke with a start, wondering where she was. The light was on and she was still

177

fully clothed. She looked at her watch. It was only eleven-fifteen. She sat up. And she remembered. The letter. What a ridiculous thing to do. She couldn't possibly send a letter like that. What was she thinking? How stupid! She hurried from her room and down the stairs to the hall table. The letter wasn't there. Perhaps her mother had removed it for some reason. She felt slightly uneasy as she approached the kitchen where she found her mother making a bedtime drink.

'I thought you were asleep,' her mother said.

'I was reading,' Shireen lied. 'Dad not back yet?' she asked.

'He's probably got talking to his mates down the pub,' she smiled. 'Anything to get out of packing. You know how much he hates it.'

'You haven't seen my letter around, have you?' asked Shireen, a slight tremor in her voice.

'What letter?'

'I left it on the hall table with all those others.'

Mum looked up. 'I asked your dad to post them on the way to the pub,' she said. 'He must've posted yours as well.'

Shireen paled.

Dear Shireen, he wrote.

I'm very excited. We've had a great day today. Some good Spanish friends took me to Segovia which was fantastic. Anyway, they've now suggested we all go off to Seville together. I can't wait. I've always wanted to see Andalucia . . . and particularly Seville. We're going by bus, so it should be an interesting journey. By the time you read this, I'll be there, watching all those flamenco dancers and maybe even visiting . . .

14

Shireen received Michael's letter a week later and she immediately began to panic. She'd had many sleepless nights about the letter *she'd* sent *him*, and now, knowing that it was probably sitting in Madrid waiting for his return from Seville, she felt even worse. He hadn't even seen it yet. And when he'd read it, how would he feel? She hadn't written a word to him since that night. She didn't know where to start. She'd spent most of her days and some evenings with Pedro, but always in the company of either Alison or Gavin . . . or both. She didn't want to be alone with Pedro. She missed Michael so much. She ached to see him again. But she also felt that if Pedro suddenly made any sort of romantic advance towards her, then . . .

★ ★ ★

Surprised that the phone was ringing so early in the morning, Shireen rushed to answer it, wondering if it were her parents calling from France. It was Alison, eager to talk about an idea she'd had.

'It's not even eight o'clock, Alison,' Shireen said. 'My eyes aren't open yet.'

'It's a lovely morning,' Alison rushed on. 'And as I'm not working today, why don't we take Pedro to Greenwich? I've rung Gavin and he's keen.'

Shireen liked the idea. 'You'll have to give me a couple of hours to get ready.'

'You ring Pedro and let him know,' said Alison. 'Gavin'll pick him up at ten.'

'OK.'

'And I'll come round to your place in about an hour.'

'An hour?' Shireen protested. 'I won't be ready in an hour.'

'You'll *have* to be,' Alison demanded. 'I need to talk to you before the boys arrive.'

She put down the receiver before Shireen had had a chance to reply.

★ ★ ★

Shireen slumped into a chair at the kitchen table and looked up at Alison with tears in her eyes.

'I didn't mean to hurt you,' said Alison. She knelt beside the chair and put her arm

181

around her best friend. 'It's just that Gavin was getting worried. I'm sure he's wrong, but . . . well, he asked me to talk to you about it.'

The tears began to run down Shireen's cheeks. 'He's not wrong, Alison,' she said, softly.

Alison was shocked. 'You don't mean you've got a thing about Pedro?'

'I don't know,' she sighed. She gripped Alison's hand. 'I love Michael, Alison. Really, I do. But he's not here and . . . '

'And Pedro?' Alison asked quickly. 'What does he feel about this?'

'Nothing,' said Shireen. 'I don't think Pedro has any idea how I feel about him. How can he? I'm not even sure how I feel about him *myself*. Anyway, he told me last week that he's in love with some Spanish girl. So nothing can possibly happen between us. Thank goodness.' The tears flowed faster. 'Oh Alison,' she sobbed. 'If only Michael was here. If only he hadn't gone away.'

'He'll be back soon.' Alison tried to comfort her. 'And everything will be just as it *was*. You'll see.'

'No, it won't,' cried Shireen. 'It can't be.'

'Don't be silly,' said Alison. 'Of course it can.'

'But you don't understand.' Shireen wiped her tears on a crumpled Kleenex.

Alison noted just how serious Shireen looked. This was something terrible, she was sure. 'What is it?' she asked, concerned. 'Tell me, Shireen. What don't I understand?'

'I've done something very silly,' Shireen explained. 'And I'm in a bit of a mess about it.'

'Tell me.'

'About a week ago, I wrote a letter to Michael,' she sobbed, 'and . . . Oh God, I wish I hadn't.'

'What sort of letter?' enquired Alison. 'What do you mean?'

The doorbell rang.

'Oh, no!' gasped Shireen.

'That's them,' said Alison. 'Look, I'll open the door while you go up to the bathroom and sort yourself out. You don't want them to see you in that state. We'll talk later, eh?'

Shireen hurriedly left the room while Alison went to open the front door.

★ ★ ★

As the bus pulled into Seville, Michael was horrified. The unattractive blocks of flats which littered the skyline weren't quite what he'd expected to see. However, the walk to Conchita and Juan's grandparents' house soon changed his opinion of the city. Every corner they turned brought more and more delights: elegant old houses with patios and courtyards filled with all kinds of brightly-coloured, exotic plants. The streets were lined with small orange trees, and the people going about their daily business beneath the bright blue, cloudless sky, seemed happy and content.

They walked to the Plaza España and across the park, passing the many fountains and palms, which were filled with cooing white doves . . . and on to the large white house where the Spanish flag flew above its portal.

'This is it,' said Conchita. She threw her bag over one shoulder and grabbed Michael's hand, dragging him excitedly along the path towards the smiling, grey-haired woman, standing on the steps which led to the front door, arms opened wide, waiting to greet her grandchildren. Juan overtook them, leaping up the steps and tightly hugging his grandma.

As Michael was introduced, the old woman kissed him on both cheeks, spoke rapidly in undecipherable Spanish and beckoned him into her palatial home, where he was given a plate of soup and crusty bread accompanied by a small glass of sherry. Having spoken in his now much-improved Spanish to Juan and Conchita's parents and grandparents, he was shown to a dark and cool, high-ceilinged bedroom where he was left to make himself comfortable before taking a quick tour around the city.

★ ★ ★

They arrived at Greenwich station around eleven o'clock and walked towards the market, where they examined the clothes, the bric-à-brac and the vulgar pieces of tourists' memorabilia. The sky was a cloudless, bright blue, as it had been for most of this exceptionally warm British summer, and all four wore just T-shirts and shorts.

Alison had felt disturbed throughout the journey, wondering what exactly Shireen had put in the letter to Michael. She'd glanced across the train carriage at her from time to time, giving her a reassuring smile and hoping that there would be some time during the day when they could talk. Shireen too was desperate, but she knew that her full confession to Alison would have to wait until after the trip. Maybe they'd be able to talk later that evening, if, somehow, they could persuade the boys to go elsewhere and leave them alone for a few hours.

'Here, this'll look really good on you,' laughed Gavin as he picked up a bright pink, wide-brimmed hat from one of the market stalls. He turned and placed it on Shireen's head, much to the annoyance of the vendor who realized they had no intention of buying anything.

'Better on me,' said Pedro as he grabbed the hat and placed it on his own head. 'A pink sombrero.'

As they all hooted with laughter, the vendor stepped forward and gently removed the hat from Pedro's head, placing it back on the stall.

They strolled on towards the *Cutty Sark* where Gavin, having read notes on the great sailing vessel from a small tourists' handbook, passed the information on to Pedro.

'I hope you're listening to this too, girls,' Gavin said with a grin. 'We don't want Pedro thinking you're two little English ignoramuses, do we?'

Alison laughed and took Gavin's arm, gently propelling him towards the river's barrier, where the four of them leaned over the rail and watched the swans gliding up the Thames towards Tower Bridge.

'Aren't they beautiful?' said Shireen.

'Yes. And they mate for life, you know,' Gavin replied as he lovingly gripped Alison's hand. 'Unlike many humans, when swans get together, it really is 'till death us do part'.'

Shireen sighed. 'What a lovely thought. I bet one of them won't be flying off to Spain and leaving the other one behind, though,' she added.

The others fell silent.

★ ★ ★

They walked into Greenwich Park and stopped outside the Observatory, studying the Greenwich Mean Time line.

Shireen grinned at Pedro. 'I hope you don't want an explanation of how the world's time is all measured from here,' she said. 'Because I wouldn't know where to start.'

'Don't worry,' Pedro grinned back. 'I know all about it . . . *and* I've read about your millennium celebrations.' He laughed. 'I wonder how much you can tell me about Madrid's Puerta Del Sol?'

They all looked at each other, blankly.

'Not a lot,' said Gavin.

Pedro beamed. 'As I thought,' he said. 'English ignoramus.'

Alison screeched with laughter and pointed at Gavin. 'There! You ignoramus. It's not just me and Shireen.'

'Right!' said Gavin. 'Calling me names, eh?' He smirked mischievously. 'See these?' He held up his fingers in front of her face.

'Yes?' she said, smiling at him. 'They're really bony, aren't they?'

'They make the most wonderful tickling machine, though,' he added.

'Don't you dare!' she shrieked.

He leapt at her and she sped away from him, screaming and laughing loudly. He chased after her, racing along the path and

188

across the field, where they caused a group of Japanese tourists to turn and laugh at the antics of these young English lovers.

Catching up with her, he pulled her down on to the grass and lay on top of her, gripping her tightly with one hand as he lifted the other hand, ready to tickle her.

'Please, don't, Gavin!' she yelped. 'I can't stand being tickled. It hurts.'

He stopped, lowered his hand and looked into her eyes. 'Would I do anything to hurt you?' he asked, softly.

She whispered back, 'I hope not.'

He pressed his lips to hers and kissed her, passionately.

Pedro and Shireen, who'd been following them across the field, suddenly stopped in their tracks and sat where they were.

'I think they'd be better off without us, don't you?' said Pedro as he and Shireen gazed down towards the Maritime Museum and at the magnificent views of London, sprawled out beyond it.

An infant whooped joyfully as he raced by them, holding on tightly to the strings of a small kite.

Shireen was lost in thought.

'Are you all right?' Pedro asked her.

'I'm fine,' she lied.

★　★　★

Having lazed in the park all day, the four left by the top gate leading to Blackheath where the fair-ground, with its flashing lights and loud music, looked inviting.

Feeling hungry, they bought burgers and chips and wandered around the rides, trying to decide which were the most appealing.

'Oh, look!' exclaimed Alison, as she noted the row of teddy bears sitting on a high shelf behind one of the stalls. 'I want one!' she cried childlike . . . and with a twinkle in her eye, she added, 'Will you win me one, Gavin?'

They all laughed.

Gavin tutted and smiled. 'How do you expect me to win one of those?' he asked. He eyed the pile of tin cans which had to be knocked down by the throwing of three tiny, soft beanbags. 'Nobody ever wins on those things.'

'Half those cans will be stuck down,' Pedro agreed.

The stallholder approached; a swarthy youth wearing a large gold earring. 'No, they ain't,' he said, aggressively. 'People only say they're *stuck* down when they ain't got the strength to *knock* 'em down.'

'I'll have a go,' Gavin said immediately.

He paid his money, picked up the three bean-bags and hurled each one at the centre pile of tin cans. The first two throws were very successful, to squeals of delight from Shireen and Alison. The third beanbag hit the cans with great force, but they refused to budge.

'Told you,' Gavin whispered. 'It's impossible.'

The stallholder approached them with three more beanbags. 'Why don't you 'ave a go?' he asked Pedro. 'You're probably stronger than yer mate!'

'I don't think so,' Pedro grinned.

'Go on, Pedro,' said Gavin. 'It's probably tactics rather than strength.'

Pedro laughed loudly. 'Oh, sure!' He paid for the beanbags and hurled them at the reset pile of tin cans.

On the third throw, the last of the remaining cans tumbled over with a crash.

Gavin was shocked. Pedro beamed and punched the air. And the two girls leapt up and down, screeching excitedly.

The stallholder picked up one of the teddy bears and handed it to Pedro. 'Told yer!' he said, with a grin. 'You're tougher than yer mate!'

Pedro immediately handed the teddy bear to Alison.

'For you,' he said.

'And now . . . ,' said Shireen, dramatically, 'the big wheel! Who thinks they're brave enough?'

'Why not?' replied Alison. She put her arm through Shireen's and both girls wandered across the fair towards the big wheel, leaving the boys to trail behind them.

'Are you OK?' Alison asked, quietly.

'Not really,' replied Shireen. 'But we can't talk about it now. Tonight, hopefully.' She sighed deeply. 'I can't believe I've been so stupid.'

'Whatever it is,' said Alison, 'I'm sure it can't be as bad as you think.'

She stopped suddenly, when she felt Gavin's hand ruffle her hair from behind.

'I like to rock the carriage,' he lied. 'So I hope you're not going to embarrass me by screaming.'

She smiled at him with a twinkle in her eye. 'Likewise!' she replied.

★ ★ ★

As Pedro and Shireen climbed into a carriage on the big wheel, Shireen was quiet.

Pedro gently took her hand. 'Are you all right?' he asked.

She smiled at him and tightly gripped on to his fingers as their carriage rose in the air a few metres and then stopped. She waved down to Alison and Gavin who climbed into the carriage below them.

As the ride began, Pedro, never fond of heights, wrapped his arm around Shireen. They gazed down at the other fairground rides and the caravans and the people, all beginning to shrink in size.

Alison sat the teddy bear on the seat beside them as she cuddled up to Gavin.

'I hate these things,' she said, half-giggling, though fear was written in her eyes.

Gavin laughed. 'Me too.'

'Then why did you come on it?' asked Alison, surprised.

'I thought *you* wanted to,' he said. 'I

would never have come on here otherwise.'

She snuggled up closer and sighed
contentedly. 'You'll be telling me next that
you'd walk through fire for me,' she said.

His sigh echoed hers. 'I probably
would,' he replied.

★ ★ ★

Alison constantly watched the clock,
wondering how she could persuade Gavin
and Pedro to leave . . . and allow her some
time with Shireen. It was eleven o'clock
already. On returning to Shireen's house,
they'd all agreed to go in for a quick cup
of coffee. But that was three hours ago.
And now, engrossed in conversation, the
boys appeared to have no intention of
leaving.

'Shall I make some more coffee?'
Shireen asked, finally.

Alison shook her head and yawned. 'Not
for me. I'll help you wash these mugs up.
I've got to be home soon. I'm working
tomorrow.'

'I've got a better idea,' suggested Pedro.
'Gavin can take you home, Alison, and I'll
stay and help Shireen wash up.'

Shireen was quick to respond. 'No. Don't worry about that, Pedro,' she said. 'Gavin can take you home too. I don't need any help to wash up a few mugs.'

Gavin looked at Alison. He didn't want to leave Pedro alone with Shireen. But he didn't know how to get the young, handsome Spaniard to leave, without causing offence. Alison too, felt helpless. She didn't know how to handle the situation.

'I insist,' said Pedro. 'I will enjoy it. I never have to wash up anything in Madrid.' He gave a broad smile. 'The servants do it for me.'

Alison looked at Shireen who shrugged, resignedly.

'I'll give you a call tomorrow, Shireen,' she said pointedly. 'As soon as I've finished work.'

And as she and Gavin left, she turned back to see the haunted look in Shireen's eyes.

★ ★ ★

Juan decided to stay and talk to his relatives as Conchita showed Michael some of the more important sights of

Seville. They gazed up at the Giralda, the incredible Moorish bell tower, before entering the cathedral to inspect the tomb of Christopher Columbus. They strolled along the palm-tree-lined river, where the many horse-drawn carriages carried excited tourists. Then they headed on towards Carmen's famous tobacco factory, returning via the gardens of the Alcazar Real which were filled with gigantic palms and fruit trees, orange, lemon and banana. Here they sat on a stone bench, listening to the fountains splashing into the pond beside them, where dozens of fish rose to the surface devouring pieces of bread being thrown to them by a small gypsy boy. The boy's father smiled through tobacco-stained teeth as he played a flamenco song on his guitar, watching another of his children, a pretty girl no older than four, dancing and swirling around as she clacked with confidence on a pair of bright red castanets.

'This was Pedro's favourite place,' sighed Conchita as she threw back her head and held her face to the evening sun.

'It's beautiful,' said Michael. 'And it's so exciting.'

Conchita shrugged. 'For me, it's sad.

Full of memories.'

Michael took her hand and squeezed it affectionately. 'But it doesn't have to be like that, Conchita,' he said. 'If you and Pedro still love each other, then it's ridiculous to be separated. I know you don't want to upset your parents, but it's *your* life. And if being apart from Pedro makes you miserable, then you must stand up to them.'

Conchita looked at her watch. 'We must go,' she said. 'It's nine o'clock and we're meeting the family for dinner.'

★   ★   ★

In a quiet courtyard at the back of a small bar, the family sat around a long wooden table, chatting and sipping at sangría as they waited for the bartender to bring them some tapas and bread as a starter.

Michael looked up at the night sky, packed to bursting with the brightest of stars. The patio walls were covered with posters depicting famous bullfighters, both modern heroes and those from yesteryear.

'Is bullfighting still popular here?' he asked.

'Very,' said Conchita. 'My grandparents

go every Sunday and my parents often go to see it in Madrid.'

'And you?' asked Michael.

'I love it,' Conchita replied.

Michael was surprised. 'But it's so barbaric,' he said.

Conchita smiled. 'You English!' she said. 'You're such hypocrites. You condemn the bullfight. Then you race through the English countryside on horse-back and watch as dogs rip foxes into little pieces.'

Michael was offended. 'Don't you think that's a great generalization? *I* don't support fox-hunting, no more than I support the murdering of bulls.'

'I agree, Michael,' said Juan as he took another sip of *sangría*. 'Not all Spanish support the bull-fight. I think it's repugnant.'

Conchita's mother laughed. 'Juan was always different. He always covered his eyes when the bull was killed. Unlike Pedro.'

'Pedro liked the bullfight?' asked Michael, sounding surprised.

'He would never miss it,' Conchita's father said. 'He and Conchita would often go to the bullring in Madrid and he loved to come here to Seville because they have some of the best bullfights in the world.'

'I wonder how my little Pedro is?' said Conchita's grandmother. 'I hope he's enjoying England.'

'He's having a wonderful time, Grandma,' Conchita replied confidently. 'He's really enjoying it there.'

Michael almost choked on his drink. He stared incredulously at Conchita, who returned his stare with a nervous flicker of a smile. Juan looked across at Michael, wide-eyed with disbelief.

'So, he's written to you?' asked Conchita's mother. 'I'm so pleased. I still can't believe that you stopped seeing him.'

'I thought you were made for each other,' added her father. 'The perfect couple.'

Grandma looked concerned as she reached across the table and took Conchita's hand. 'What *did* go wrong?' she asked. 'I was very upset to hear that your relationship was over. He's such a nice boy, Conchita.'

Conchita forced a smile as she quickly wiped away a tear with her free hand.

'If you can discover the truth, Mama,' said Conchita's mother, 'then you're a better woman than I.'

'I really would like to change the subject,' pleaded Conchita. 'Pedro and I are finished as a couple. I hope we will continue to be friends, but we can never be really close again.' She took out her handkerchief and dabbed her eyes. 'Will you excuse me for a moment?' she said as she left the table and headed towards the bar.

Michael watched her go, shocked at the realization that Conchita's parents had nothing to do with the break-up.

Why had she lied? What *was* the truth?

15

The family strolled back through the winding Sevillano streets, and on reaching the house they said their goodnights. When Juan suggested that he and Michael sit in the garden for a while, sipping some cool lemonade, Michael readily agreed. It was far too humid to sleep. Even though it was nearing midnight, sweat was popping from beneath his blond hair and trickling down his cheeks. Conchita joined them, sitting on the old garden swing, which had been placed there years before for the enjoyment of Juan and Conchita when they were still toddlers.

Juan and Michael flopped on to the small wrought-iron bench, facing the swing.

'So, tell me,' said Juan, sounding annoyed with his sister, 'what was that all about? *Has* Pedro been writing to you?'

Conchita looked down at her feet as she swung gently to and fro.

'Conchita?' he said. 'I'm confused. Please, tell me.'

'No,' she replied in a whisper. 'He hasn't written to me.'

'I don't understand,' said Michael. 'Then why did you say he had?'

She looked up at them and began to raise her voice. 'Because I'm sick of the questions. I'm sick of being reprimanded by everyone for ending the relationship with Pedro. I thought if I said that we were still friends, then the matter would be dropped . . . at least for this evening.'

Juan sipped on his lemonade. 'But now Mama and Papa will expect Pedro to visit us when he returns,' he said. 'And that will never happen, will it?'

Conchita rose from the swing and looked sadly at Juan. 'No, he'll never visit.' Tears filled her eyes. 'I wish he *would*. I miss him. I wish he *had* written to me. But he hasn't. And he won't, unless . . . '

'Unless *you* write to *him*,' interrupted Michael.

'I can't,' she said. 'It's too late, Michael. I can't do it. I've tried. But I can't.'

Leaving the two boys staring after her, she walked slowly across the garden towards the house.

Juan and Michael sat in silence for a while, watching the stars and listening to

202

the sound of the cicadas.

Juan finally broke the silence. 'I hate to see her so unhappy. She was always such fun. When she and Pedro were together there was so much laughter. They were really good company.'

Michael shrugged. 'It's such a waste. When two people are in love like that, it seems nonsense to spend their time apart.'

Juan smiled. 'Like you and your English girl-friend.'

'Shireen? That's different,' said Michael. 'We're only apart for five weeks. We'll be back together soon.'

'But you are unhappy without her.'

'Yes, but I'm happy to have seen Spain.'

'But you'd be happier to see Spain if she were with you.'

'Of course,' said Michael. 'I've got this great fear that when I return to London, she'll have found someone else.'

'Then perhaps you shouldn't stay away from her for quite so long,' Juan lectured him.

Michael sighed. 'I've been wondering about that. I think about her every day. I go to sleep with pictures of her in my head. And everything I see or do I want to share with her. I keep wanting to turn to her and say, 'Look at that, Shireen,' or, 'Isn't that beautiful, Shireen?' This visit is so exciting for me, Juan, and yet it's a part of my life that she can never share. Even though I write and tell her everything in detail, she can never *really* be part of it.'

'If I had someone to love,' said Juan, 'I would never put myself through this torture. There's Pedro in England and Conchita here . . . a thousand miles apart. And the same for you and Shireen.'

'But hopefully, when I return, Shireen will be waiting for me,' replied Michael.

'*Hopefully*,' said Juan, pointedly.

'But unless Conchita tells your parents to stop interfering in her life, then *she* and *Pedro* will never get back together.'

'My parents?' asked Juan, surprised. 'What have my parents got to do with it?'

'Conchita's told me,' replied Michael. 'And so has Santi. Your mother and father don't approve of Pedro as a partner for Conchita because he's abandoned his Catholic faith.'

Juan was horrified. 'They told you that?'

'Yes. I was very surprised when they spoke of Pedro so affectionately after all they'd done to ruin the relationship.'

'But it isn't true,' said Juan. 'My parents

and my grandparents love Pedro. Santi was definitely mistaken. It was Conchita's decision. It was *she* who was distressed because Pedro wouldn't return to the church. Conchita was thinking of marriage and she felt that her future had to be spent with someone who shared her faith. It's Conchita's decision alone. My parents had nothing to do with it.'

Michael felt angry. 'Then she doesn't love him. Not really,' he said bluntly.

'Oh, I think you're wrong,' said Juan. 'She loves him very much.'

'No,' Michael said softly. 'She doesn't. She wants to control him. True love is unconditional. Conchita doesn't love Pedro for what he *is*, but for what she would *like* him to be.'

'Yes. I understand what you're saying.' Juan nodded solemnly. 'My faith is very important to me, but if I fell in love with someone who didn't share the same faith, then I hope I would respect that person's way of life.'

'You're right,' said Conchita. Stepping from the shadows, where she'd listened to the whole conversation, she approached them. She knelt in front of the bench and looked up at Michael.

'I'm sorry, Conchita,' said Michael. 'It's got nothing to do with me. I have no right . . . '

She gently placed a hand on his knee. 'You have *every* right, Michael. You're my friend, I hope.'

'Conchita,' he softly pleaded. 'Write to him. Tell him how you feel. Don't throw your love away.'

Juan agreed. 'Remember all those wonderful times you and Pedro had together. I've never seen two happier people, Conchita. You may still have your differences, but that doesn't stop you loving each other for what you are. At least *try* to make it work.'

Conchita smiled. 'I've been thinking about it very deeply,' she said. 'I began to write to him when we returned from Segovia, but I tore the letter up. I couldn't express myself properly on paper. I'm not good at writing love letters.'

'Well then, *call* him,' said Michael. 'Talk to him.' He looked at his watch. 'It's twelve-forty-five,' he added. 'So it's eleven-forty-five in London. He may still be up, talking to my parents. Call him *now*.'

Conchita grinned broadly. She suddenly felt so happy, so confident about the future. 'Why not?' she said. She grabbed Michael's hand and pulled him to his feet. 'Tell me the number.'

The three of them hurried up to the house. 'I'll dial it for you,' said Michael.

★ ★ ★

Pedro clumsily wiped each of the mugs which Shireen handed to him.

'You're not very good at this, are you?' Shireen laughed.

'Not very,' grinned Pedro. 'I haven't had much practice.'

'You'd better get used to it,' she said. 'You may not always have servants.'

'I don't want them,' replied Pedro. 'When I marry, I want a small house with a beautiful wife who will do everything for me. I wouldn't want to have maids getting in the way all the time.'

Shireen dropped the mug she was holding, back into the soapy water. 'Oh, excuse me?' she said, harshly. 'You want a wife to do everything for you? How about you and your wife working together? Or *you* doing everything for *her*?'

Pedro laughed. 'But I will have to work. She will stay at home and have babies and look after the house.'

Shireen couldn't believe what she was hearing. 'And suppose your wife wants a career?'

Pedro eyes twinkled. He was enjoying the joke. 'But she can't,' he said. 'I can't have the babies, can I? That will be her job. I will have to go to work.'

She said it without thinking, 'And how did Conchita cope with that idea? Is that why she left you?'

He looked at her, sadly.

'I'm sorry,' she said.

He tried to smile, quickly grabbing another mug from the draining-board. 'I was only making fun,' he informed her. 'I was joking.'

'Oh,' she said. She felt deeply embarrassed. 'I'm sorry,' she repeated as she continued to wash up.

'Sorry for what? You don't have to be sorry.'

She turned from the sink to face him. 'Pedro . . . ?'

'Yes?'

'Tell me why it ended,' she said. 'Why did you and Conchita separate? If you still love each other as you say you do, then I don't understand.'

'Why do you want to know?' he asked her, softly.

'Because I'm selfish,' she replied. 'Because, if I'm truthful, I'm only thinking about myself.'

'I don't know what you mean,' he said. 'Thinking about yourself? What do you mean by that?'

'Because if two people love each other and yet their relationship comes to an end . . . '

'Yes?'

'Then that could happen to Michael and me, couldn't it?' she said, fearfully.

Pedro smiled. 'No,' he said. 'It's not the same situation at all. Conchita and I have a deep difference of opinion that keeps us apart.'

'Such as?' she enquired.

'I'd better go,' he said. 'It's getting late. Michael's parents will be worried about me.'

Shireen looked up at the clock on the kitchen wall. 'It's a quarter to twelve,' she said. 'Perhaps you'd better call them and tell them where you are.'

'Perhaps I should,' he agreed.

★ ★ ★

'It's engaged,' said Michael, sounding surprised. He wondered who his parents could be talking to at such a late hour.

Conchita was distressed. Having finally plucked up the courage to speak to Pedro, she now had to put everything on hold. The adrenalin was surging through her body. Her heart was pounding.

'I'll try again,' said Michael as he redialled the number. He waited. 'Aah, it's ringing,' he said.

Conchita's mouth was dry. How would she start the conversation? What was she going to say?

She and Juan listened as Michael spoke to his mother, quickly relating tales of Madrid, Segovia, Seville and his new-found friends.

'Can I speak to Pedro?' he asked eventually.

There was a pause.

'Oh!' he said. 'Really?'

Having wished his mother goodnight, he put down the receiver with a trembling hand.

'What the matter?' asked Conchita, sounding very concerned.

'Pedro's not there,' he informed her. 'He

hasn't got back yet.'

Michael knew that Shireen's parents would be in France by now. Pedro and Shireen were together . . . alone . . . at her house. And it was almost midnight.

16

Having stacked the mugs and wiped down the kitchen surfaces, Pedro sat over yet another cup of coffee and talked as he hadn't talked for months. Shireen was a good listener and it felt good to unburden himself in this way.

'Why don't you write to her?' Shireen asked. 'Tell her everything you've told me.'

He shrugged. 'She'd probably just throw the letter away.'

'But she may *not*, Pedro.' Shireen was doing her best to sound positive. 'Surely it's worth a try? If you both love each other, it seems such a waste to let it all go.'

'I wouldn't know where to start.' He smiled. 'I've never been good at writing love letters.'

'I'll help you,' she said. She leapt up from the table. 'Why don't I get some paper? We could do it together; put down all your thoughts in writing.'

She suddenly thought about the last letter she'd sent to Michael and she felt the palms of her hands begin to sweat.

Here she was, giving advice to a friend; helping him to write a love letter, when she feared that the last one *she'd* written had been a total disaster. She wished that she could explain everything to Pedro: how sick she was feeling inside and how she feared that her final letter to Michael might have ended their relationship.

With a trembling hand, she placed the paper and a pen in front of him. 'Let's start,' she said. 'Dear Conchita . . . '

★　★　★

Conchita quietly left the house, looking back at the lamp glowing softly through her bedroom window. The other rooms were in darkness, its inhabitants sleeping soundly. She strolled very slowly into the town, passing many who, like herself, couldn't sleep on this humid Andalucian night.

She gazed up at the moon, almost full, and at the thousands of stars which surrounded it, and she thought of the nights that she and Pedro had strolled hand in hand beneath this very sky and had talked about their future together. It had taken hours to compose the letter which she was gripping tightly in her hand and yet she still wasn't sure if she'd have the courage to post it. She wanted Pedro back. Badly. There'd been no happiness in her life since he'd left. And Michael was right. True love shouldn't carry conditions. She'd loved Pedro for what he was and she had no right to impose her ideals on him.

When she'd asked Michael for the address, both he and Juan had seemed delighted. Then, shut away in her room, she'd written what she really felt for Pedro. But could she actually send the letter? She reached the mail box, hovered for a while . . . and then walked on. She stopped and turned back. Then, with great trepidation, she sealed the envelope with a kiss . . . and sent it on its way to London.

* * *

Alison put out her hand and gripped Shireen's. 'Tell me,' she said. 'I can't help you if I don't know what's going on, can I?'

As the tears rolled, Shireen explained how she'd been confused about her feelings for Pedro and about the letter she'd sent to Michael.

Alison gasped. 'Oh Shireen. You didn't!'

'Nothing happened between me and Pedro,' she said. 'Really. He didn't even know how I felt. Thank goodness he didn't because I don't feel that way any more. He's just a good friend, Alison, and he's totally in love with his Spanish girlfriend.'

'But why did you send the letter?' asked Alison. 'I can't believe you did that.'

'Me neither,' sobbed Shireen. 'It was the most stupid thing I've ever done. I was just feeling so lost without Michael and so muddled up about everything.' She took out a Kleenex and dabbed her eyes. 'Oh Alison. What am I going to do?'

'You should've trusted me,' Alison scolded her. 'I'm your best friend, Shireen. You should've told me what you were going through and we could've talked. Then none of this would've happened.'

'You were too busy,' Shireen replied. 'What with work and Gavin and — '

Alison was upset. 'But we're friends, Shireen. We know everything about each other. I would've found time for you, no matter what else was going on in my life.'

'I know, I know,' said Shireen.

Alison gripped Shireen's hand more tightly. 'We tell each other everything. We always have.' She immediately felt guilty. She hadn't told Shireen of the relief she'd felt when Pedro had arrived on the scene. It had meant that, now they were a foursome again, Alison would have Gavin's full attention. She wouldn't have to share it with Shireen.

'Perhaps we haven't been as open with each other as we should've been,' added Alison, sadly. 'And we *must* be, Shireen. In future. Neither Gavin nor Michael must come between us, no matter how much we love them. Our friendship is too important.'

'Yes,' agreed Shireen. 'It is.'

Both girls stood and hugged each other. 'Now,' Alison said softly, 'what are we going to do about this letter you've sent to Michael?'

*   *   *

Pedro rang his mother as soon as she'd arrived home from work.

'And how's the English?' she asked.

'Good,' he said. 'It's getting better all the time. In fact, it's so good that I don't think I need to spend the full five weeks here.'

She laughed. 'You're feeling homesick?'

'A bit.'

'And you're missing your mother.'

'That too,' he laughed back.

'Or could it be that you're missing someone else?' she asked.

'You haven't seen her, have you?'

'No. Not for a few days.' She wondered if she should tell Pedro that Conchita was in Seville with her brother . . . and Michael, but fearing that it might hurt him if she delivered such a message over the phone, she decided to change the subject. 'So tell me all about London. Is it raining there as usual?'

'It's been very warm and sunny, actually,' he replied. 'Though not as hot as Madrid, I'm sure. Listen,' he added, 'will you do me a big favour, without asking any questions?'

'Now, that depends,' she replied.

'Is there a letter there for Michael, postmarked from London?'

'Yes. What about it?' she was curious.

'Will you destroy it, please?'

'Destroy it? I can't do that,' she said.

'Please, Mama,' he said. 'You'll be doing a very kind service to two people. You may even prevent a relationship from ending in tears.'

'It's that serious?'

'It's that serious.'

'Don't tell your father what I've done,' she said.

He laughed. 'I promise.'

'So, are you staying the full course?' she asked. 'We can hardly ask Michael to vacate your room. Shall I ask the maid to make up a spare bed?'

'Give me a few days to think about it,' he replied.

★   ★   ★

Michael returned from Seville, looking forward to opening the several letters that would surely be waiting for him. He was disturbed when Pedro's mother, somewhat guiltily, informed him that there hadn't been any post from London.

Throughout the morning he couldn't stop fretting, wondering if Shireen had given up on him. He couldn't help worrying that she might have found someone else. And it crossed his mind that that someone else might be Pedro.

Conchita noted how glum he looked as

soon as he walked into the Torito later that evening.

'You were very keen to advise *me*, Michael,' she said with a comforting smile. 'But are you as good at receiving advice?'

'Tell me,' he said.

'Call her. There's a telephone just outside the bar. Call her and tell her you love her. Ask her if there's anything wrong.'

* * *

'No, there's nothing wrong,' she said. Her heart was pounding. 'Oh, it's so wonderful to hear your voice, Michael.'

'But you haven't written,' he said, plaintively.

She beamed. So the letter *had* been destroyed as Pedro had promised. 'I didn't see the point,' she said. 'You were in Seville. I didn't have an address there.'

'Do you miss me?' he asked.

'I miss you like crazy, Michael.'

'I miss you too,' he said. 'It's beautiful here, but it's pointless when I can't share it with you.'

'Only another couple of weeks,' she mused, 'and we'll be together again.'

'Maybe sooner,' he replied.

She was startled. 'Sooner?'

'What would you say if I told you I was thinking of coming back earlier?'

'Are you kidding?'

'I'm deadly serious.'

'When?' she asked, excitedly.

'As soon as I can get a flight.'

She sighed. 'Oh Michael!'

'Would you meet me at the airport?'

'Try keeping me away.'

★ ★ ★

The doorbell rang just as she put down the phone. She shrieked with joy and raced along the hall. She was expecting Alison to call round and she couldn't wait to tell her the news. She was surprised to see Pedro, standing on the step, beaming at her and holding up a letter.

'I've got wonderful news,' he said.

She grinned at him. 'You and me both. Come in. I'll put the kettle on.'

★ ★ ★

'Well?' asked Conchita. 'Was she there?'

'Yes,' said Michael. 'And everything's

fine.' He paused, took Conchita's hand and stared into the dark green eyes. 'I think I'm going home,' he said. 'I can't bear to be without her any longer.'

She smiled at him. 'A good idea.'

'Perhaps Pedro will do the same,' he said, only half-convinced.

'He will,' she replied, confidently.

He gazed at her. 'Is there something you're not telling me?'

She laughed. 'I wrote to him from Seville as you suggested,' she said. 'I told him that I wanted to start again. With no conditions.'

Michael flung his arms around her and whooped loudly. 'Well done!'

'And even better than that,' she added. 'Look.' From her pocket she took out a letter. 'He must have written to me at the same time.' Her green eyes suddenly misted over. 'He misses me, Michael. He wants to come home as soon as possible, to try and patch things up between us.'

'He won't have to try very hard, will he?' grinned Michael.

'There's no patching up to be done,' she said. 'He's done nothing wrong. I want Pedro for Pedro's sake. I love him just the way he is.'

★ ★ ★

Conchita stood silently at the arrival gate, waiting for the London to Madrid flight. Lost in her thoughts, past, present and future, she was almost oblivious to the conversation between Michael and Pedro's parents.

'Thank you for everything, Antonio,' said Michael. 'You and Suzana have made me so welcome.'

'Any time, Michael,' Antonio replied.

'And if you want to return and bring Shireen with you,' added Suzana, 'just give us a call. *Our* house is *your* house.'

Conchita gave a gasp and a tiny squeal as she saw Pedro pass through passport control.

'He's here,' she yelled.

'I'll go,' said Michael. 'I have to board in ten minutes. He shook Antonio's hand and kissed Suzana on both cheeks. 'Thanks again.'

He gently placed an arm around Conchita's neck, kissed her quickly on the cheek and without waiting for a response, he hurried away towards the departure gate.

'I *told* you it was the first thing we'd do when I got home from Spain,' said Michael.

'Our pact,' added Gavin.

The fire crackled and burned even brighter than the first fire they'd built here.

'Let's just hope that Gavin's car starts this time,' laughed Shireen as she huddled closer to Michael, watching the sparks fly.

'It wouldn't matter to me if it *didn't* start,' said Michael. 'Who wants to go home?'

'I wouldn't mind staying here for ever and ever,' agreed Gavin. 'Just like this. Me and Alison. And you two. Lost in our own little Heaven.' He sighed deeply. 'I bet you're all glad that I showed you this place, aren't you?'

'We certainly are, Gavin,' Michael grinned. 'Perhaps we should come back here at this time every year. On our anniversaries.' He laughed. 'An annual trip to Bluebell Wood.'

Alison looked around her and smiled. 'Not a lot of bluebells, are there?'

'Does it bother you?' asked Gavin.

'Not in the least,' replied Alison.

'Nor me,' added Shireen.

Michael lay down beside the glowing embers of the fire, pulled Shireen towards him and wrapped his arms around her.

'Me neither,' he said.

THE END

APL			CCS		
Cen			Ear		
Mob			Cou		
ALL			Jub		
WIL			CHE		
Aid			Bel		
Fin			Fol		
Can			STO		
TIL			HCL		